TERRY
and the Pirates
by MILTON CANIFF

NETWORK OF INTRIGUE

FLYING BUTTRESS
Classics Library

Our Story So Far...

As the Japanese invaders suffer humiliating losses inflicted by the heroic guerilla tactics of the Dragon Lady, they call on her arch-enemy Klang to help eradicate her. Klang sets a trap with dummy soldiers as bait. Our heroes, who are split between the two camps as captives, desperately try to reunite. Pat, from the invader side, is caught spying by Klang and is put in among the dummies. Terry, on the Dragon Lady's side, is the first however to suspect a trap, but seeing Pat in trouble rushes forth anyway to the rescue. As he unbinds him, Terry is hit by a bullet . . .

ISBN 0-918348-60-9
LC# 87-090446

© NBM 1988
cover designed and painted by Ray Fehrenbach

Terry & The Pirates is a registered trademark of Tribune Media Services, Inc.

THE FLYING BUTTRESS CLASSICS LIBRARY
is an imprint of:

NANTIER · BEALL · MINOUSTCHINE
Publishing co.
new york

MASTER, YOUR TROOPS RALLY ON THE HIGH GROUND OUT OF RANGE— BUT THE TWO FOREIGNERS LIE IN THE LINE OF FIRE!
ENOUGH THAT THE ARMY IS SAVED!—THE INVADER IS NOT LIKELY TO ATTACK TWO OCCIDENTALS!
8-30
THAT ACCURSED WOMAN WITHDRAWS TO SAFETY! THE AMBUSH IS BUT A FAILURE!
BUT, MASTER KLANG, IT WAS YOUR TWO SHOTS AT THE WHITE PRISONER THAT EXPOSED OUR POSITION!
Reg. U. S. Pat. Off.; Copyright, 1939, by News Syndicate Co., Inc.
FOOL—TO QUESTION THE GENERALSHIP OF THE GREAT KLANG...
CHARGE DOWN THROUGH THE DUMMY CAMP AND ROUT THE DRAGON LADY'S MINIONS! CUT THE TWO WHITE SWINE TO PIECES ON THE WAY!!
MILTON CANIFF

OBSERVE! THE ENEMY SWEEPS FROM ITS POSITION!
SO! BEGIN A REAR GUARD ACTION TO COVER OUR MAIN BODY OF TROOPS AS WE MOVE TO SAFETY DOWN THE GORGE!
8-31
KLANG'S MOB IS ROLLIN' DOWN THE HILL... LOOKS AS IF WE'RE ON THEIR MASSACRE LIST!
BEHOLD, MASTER, WE ARE NOT OPPOSED BY THE INVADER... IT IS A BANDIT ARMY! —NATIVE TRAITORS!
THAT MEANS KLANG! ARISE, MY MEN! COUNTER-CHARGE! THE DRAGON LADY WILL FIGHT THAT BEAST ANY TIME, ANYWHERE! SHOW NO MERCY! FORWARD!
Reg. U. S. Pat. Off.; Copyright, 1939, by News Syndicate Co., Inc.
MILTON CANIFF

AS KLANG'S BANDIT ARMY POURS INTO THE VALLEY, THE DRAGON LADY'S TROOPS TURN AND CHARGE... IT IS STEEL FOR STEEL—AND NO QUARTER GIVEN!
9-1
Reg. U. S. Pat. Off.; Copyright, 1939, by News Syndicate Co., Inc.
MILTON CANIFF

A BREAK! THE DRAGON LADY'S GANG PASSED US BY AND TANGLED WITH KLANG BEFORE HIS HOODLUMS COULD REACH US! THANKS, BEAUTIFUL!
THE YOUNG ONE HURT? MOVE HIM TO THE REAR WHILE THERE IS YET TIME!
9-2
OUR MEN WAVER BEFORE THE FIERCE ATTACK OF THE DRAGON LADY'S STUPID FOLLOWERS!
CALL OUR RESERVES INTO ACTION! THIS CANNOT HAPPEN TO KLANG!
WE HAVE DEALT A TELLING STROKE AND MAY NOW FALL BACK TO THE RIVER IN ALL HONOR! GIVE GROUND, BUT MAKE THE DOGS BUY IT DEARLY!
WE ARE OUTNUMBERED, HANDSOME ONE! COULD YOU SEE FIT TO CAST YOUR LOT WITH THE DRAGON LADY AGAINST THE BEAST WHO SHOT DOWN YOUR YOUNG FRIEND?
BABY, YOU'VE HAD A RECRUIT SINCE THAT BULLET HIT!
Reg. U. S. Pat. Off.; Copyright, 1939, by News Syndicate Co., Inc.
MILTON CANIFF

TERRY AND THE PIRATES
by MILTON CANIFF
Reg. U. S. Pat. Off.: Copyright, 1939, by News Syndicate Co. Inc.
TERRY IS HIT! ... RUSHING INTO THE TEETH OF KLANG'S VOLLEY, HE BURNS PAT'S BONDS WITH ONE OF THE OIL FLARES— BUT A BULLET CUTS HIM DOWN ....
THE DRAGON LADY ORDERS A CHARGE TO RESCUE TERRY AND PAT— THEN HER MEN FALL BACK TO HIGHER GROUND BEFORE KLANG'S SUPERIOR NUMBERS ...
MY MEN CAN HOLD NO LONGER! I MUST WITHDRAW! THE BEST WAY IS DOWN THE RIVER UNDER THE HIGH BRIDGE! —BUT THE PATH DOWN THE CLIFF IS NARROW— KLANG WOULD HAVE US AT HIS MERCY!
GETTING LIGHT! HAVE YOUR MEN SET UP THIS CAPTURED MACHINE GUN ON THE ROCKS OVERLOOKING THE BRIDGE ...TAKE TERRY! I'LL COVER YOUR RETREAT!
THE DRAGON LADY BARKS THE ORDER AND HER EXHAUSTED TROOPS FALL SLOWLY BACK TO THE HIGH RIVER BANK...
OBSERVE, MASTER, THE DOGS GIVE GROUND!
BUT STUBBORNLY! —WHEN THEY REACH THE BRIDGE WE CUT THEM TO PIECES!
WITH THE FULL BODY OF GUERILLAS ON THE BRIDGE, THE DRAGON LADY'S REAR GUARD CEASES FIRING AND RUNS FOR THE RIVER...
THE TIME IS NOW! CHARGE!
CONFUSED, KLANG'S LINE WAVERS UNDER PAT'S BLISTERING FIRE....
A LONE PERSON HOLDS THE BRIDGEHEAD WITH A MACHINE GUN, SIRE! IT IS THAT ACCURSED WHITE PRISONER!
SEND A DETACHMENT TO SILENCE THE LOW SWINE WHO THUS DELAYS KLANG'S VICTORY!
HURRY, BEAUTIFUL! GET MY PAL DOWN TO THAT RIVER! ... CAN'T HOLD OUT MUCH LONGER... GOT TOO MANY CUSTOMERS! LUCKY I SAVED SOME GRENADES...
...'CAUSE I DON'T WANT TO LEAVE WITHOUT PLANTING A KISS FOR YOU BOYS...
.....TO REMEMBER ME BY!!!

9-4
BEHOLD, MASTER, THE RESOURCEFUL WHITE PERSON HELD THE BRIDGE UNTIL OUR MEN WERE SAFELY OUT OF KLANG'S RANGE!
THE DRAGON LADY IS WELL AWARE OF THE ABILITIES OF THE MAN RYAN! THE CURRENT WILL CARRY HIM TO US HERE! ASSIST HIM TO SHORE!
Reg. U. S. Pat. Off.; Copyright, 1939, by News Syndicate Co., Inc.
MAY THAT AMERICAN BE TORTURED BY A THOUSAND DEVILS! HE DEMORALIZED THE MEN OF KLANG — WOUNDED MANY — AND HALTED THE PURSUIT OF THE DRAGON LADY!
AYE, MASTER KLANG, OUR MEN ARE EXHAUSTED — BUT THE ENEMY WILL BE MORE SO... THE DRAGON LADY WILL LEAVE A CLEAR TRAIL TO HER HIDING PLACE — WHITHER WE MAY REPAIR WITHOUT HASTE... AND DESTROY HER AT LEISURE!
BOMBARDMENT! STARVATION!... THEN, PRESENTLY, A SERIES OF INTERESTING EXECUTIONS OF SURVIVORS! AH, YES, A PLEASANT PROSPECT!!
MILTON CANIFF

9-5
HOW'S TERRY?
FEVERISH... BUT THE YOUNG ONE CAN ABSORB PUNISHMENT... EVEN AS YOU... TO WHOM MY ENTIRE ARMY IS DULY GRATEFUL!
GLAD TO DO ANYTHING TO CROSS UP THAT PUNK NAMED KLANG! YOU KNOW HIM, I SUPPOSE!
INDEED!
DOUBTLESS THE INVADER HAS SUBSIDIZED HIM TO FIGHT US WITH OUR OWN METHODS! HIS PARTICULAR PLEASURE WOULD BE TO ELIMINATE THE DRAGON LADY!
MILTON CANIFF
Reg. U. S. Pat. Off.; Copyright, 1939, by News Syndicate Co., Inc.
...WE CAN HARDLY COVER OUR TRAIL — WITH SO MANY WOUNDED TO TRANSPORT! MY HIDING PLACE WILL BE DISCOVERED AND BESIEGED! YOU MIGHT FIND IT WISE TO TAKE YOUR FRIENDS AND STRIKE OUT FOR SAFER PARTS!
I COULD HARDLY HELP YOU AGAINST THE INVADER — BUT AGAINST KLANG... BESIDES, I'D NEVER LET A LITTLE GAL GO HOME ALONE!

9-6
EVEN NOW, MY GENERAL, THE DRAGON LADY'S BAND LIMPS TO HER BASE — WITH MY MEN IN PURSUIT!
THE AMBUSH YOU SO ARTFULLY ARRANGED WAS NOT ENTIRELY SUCCESSFUL, THEN...?
Reg. U. S. Pat. Off.; Copyright, 1939, by News Syndicate Co., Inc.
AT THE MOMENT OF VICTORY MY MEN WERE DIVERTED FROM THEIR GOAL BY AN AMERICAN FRIEND OF THE DRAGON LADY! HE, TOO, WILL BE ELIMINATED ALONG WITH THE WOMAN!
AMERICAN SOLDIERS OF FORTUNE ARE OF NO CONCERN TO ME! YOUR TASK IS TO DESTROY THIS GUERRILLA ANNOYANCE!
THEN, IF THE GENERAL WILL BUT SUPPLY THE EQUIPMENT LISTED HERE, IT WILL REQUIRE SO LITTLE TIME TO ACHIEVE THE DESIRED END!
DOES APRIL REALLY LIKE ME?.. DID SHE MEAN IT WHEN SHE SAID I WAS BRAVE?... HAS SHE GOT A BOY FRIEND WAITIN' BACK HOME?... DOES SHE REALLY RESPECT DEETH MORE?...
RAVE ON, PAL! YOU'LL PROBABLY BE WONDERING THE SAME THINGS ALL YOUR LIFE... WHETHER YOU'RE UNCONSCIOUS OR OTHERWISE!
MILTON CANIFF

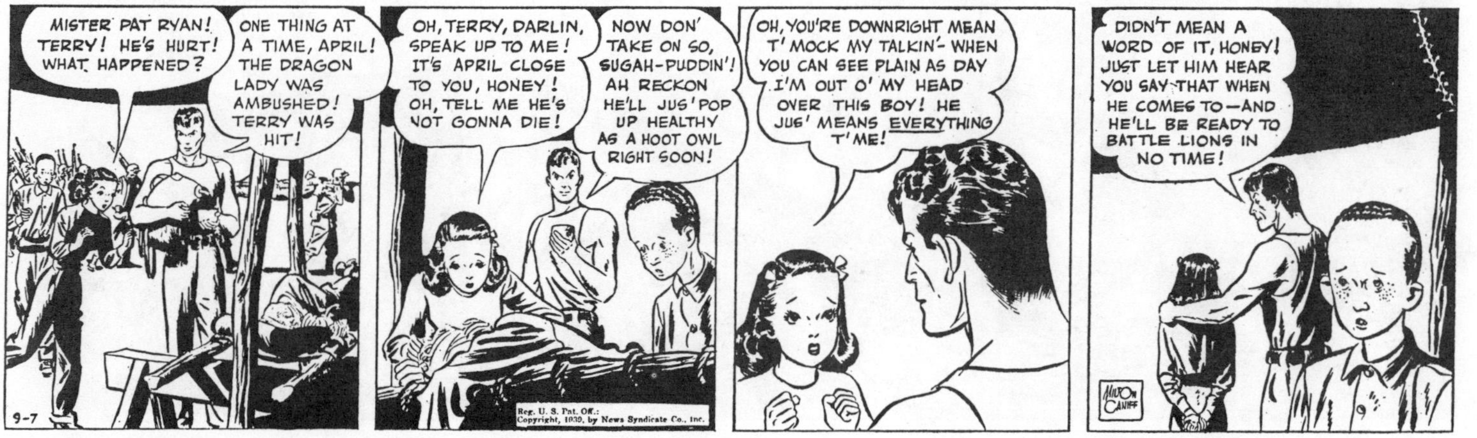
9-7
MISTER PAT RYAN! TERRY! HE'S HURT! WHAT HAPPENED?
ONE THING AT A TIME, APRIL! THE DRAGON LADY WAS AMBUSHED! TERRY WAS HIT!
OH, TERRY, DARLIN, SPEAK UP TO ME! IT'S APRIL CLOSE TO YOU, HONEY! OH, TELL ME HE'S NOT GONNA DIE!
NOW DON' TAKE ON SO, SUGAH-PUDDIN'! AH RECKON HE'LL JUS' POP UP HEALTHY AS A HOOT OWL RIGHT SOON!
Reg. U. S. Pat. Off.; Copyright, 1939, by News Syndicate Co., Inc.
OH, YOU'RE DOWNRIGHT MEAN T' MOCK MY TALKIN' — WHEN YOU CAN SEE PLAIN AS DAY I'M OUT O' MY HEAD OVER THIS BOY! HE JUS' MEANS EVERYTHING T' ME!
DIDN'T MEAN A WORD OF IT, HONEY! JUST LET HIM HEAR YOU SAY THAT WHEN HE COMES TO — AND HE'LL BE READY TO BATTLE LIONS IN NO TIME!
MILTON CANIFF

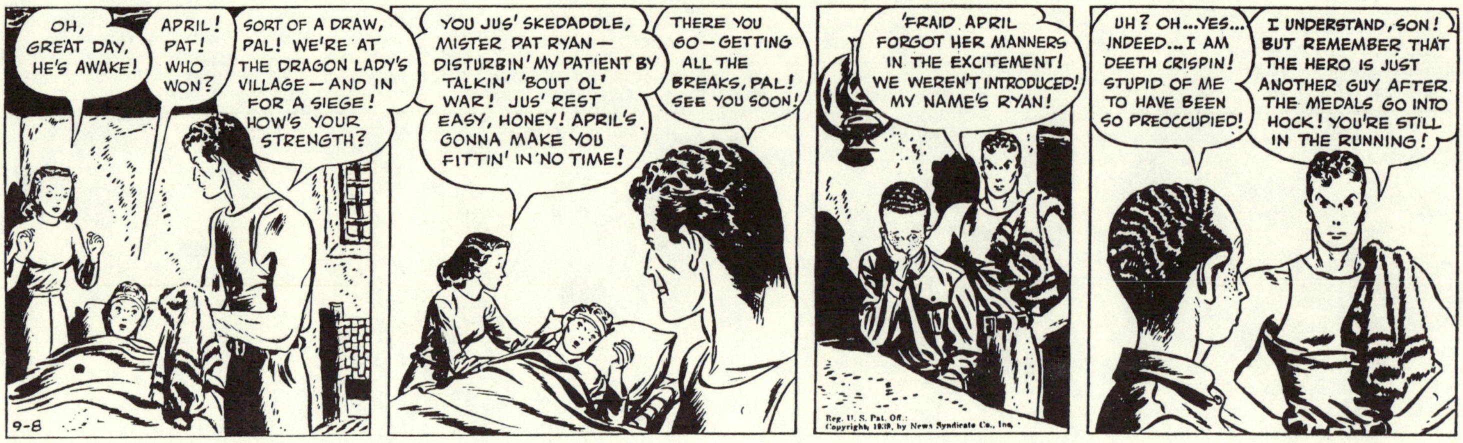
OH, GREAT DAY, HE'S AWAKE!
APRIL! PAT! WHO WON?
SORT OF A DRAW, PAL! WE'RE AT THE DRAGON LADY'S VILLAGE — AND IN FOR A SIEGE! HOW'S YOUR STRENGTH?
9-8
YOU JUS' SKEDADDLE, MISTER PAT RYAN — DISTURBIN' MY PATIENT BY TALKIN' 'BOUT OL' WAR! JUS' REST EASY, HONEY! APRIL'S GONNA MAKE YOU FITTIN' IN NO TIME!
THERE YOU GO — GETTING ALL THE BREAKS, PAL! SEE YOU SOON!
'FRAID APRIL FORGOT HER MANNERS IN THE EXCITEMENT! WE WEREN'T INTRODUCED! MY NAME'S RYAN!
Reg. U. S. Pat. Off. Copyright, 1939, by News Syndicate Co., Inc.
UH? OH...YES... INDEED...I AM DEETH CRISPIN! STUPID OF ME TO HAVE BEEN SO PREOCCUPIED!
I UNDERSTAND, SON! BUT REMEMBER THAT THE HERO IS JUST ANOTHER GUY AFTER THE MEDALS GO INTO HOCK! YOU'RE STILL IN THE RUNNING!

COUNTING THE BUTCHER'S BILL, BEAUTIFUL?
SO! WE LOST MANY MEN — AND MORE LIE WOUNDED! ALREADY MY SENTRIES REPORT KLANG'S TROOPS MASSING BEFORE THE FORTIFIED ENTRANCE TO THIS ROCKY FASTNESS!
9-9
PRETTY SLOOMY OUTLOOK, EH?
QUITE! KLANG HAS BLOCKED ALL EXITS FROM THIS VALLEY... EVEN IF WE FIGHT OUR WAY OUT WE MUST LEAVE THE WOMEN, CHILDREN AND WOUNDED TO BE SLAUGHTERED! IF WE FAIL....
AT THIS MOMENT IN THE STREET BELOW....
HAH! KLANG LAUGHS! THE DRAGON LADY CLOSES THE ENTRANCE TO HER SILLY HIDEAWAY — BUT OUR SHELLS DROP AS RAIN IN HER GARDEN! SHE WILL FIND THE SHOWER UNREFRESHING!
MILTON CANIFF
Reg. U. S. Pat. Off. Copyright, 1939, by News Syndicate Co., Inc.

TERRY AND THE PIRATES
by MILTON CANIFF
Reg. U. S. Pat. Off. Copyright, 1939, by News Syndicate Co., Inc.
JUS' YOU DON'T WORRY YOUR HEAD 'BOUT OL' WAR! APRIL'S GONNA SEE THAT YOU GET WELL! AFTER ALL, HONEY, YOU'RE MY HERO!
BUT, APRIL, THAT'S SHELL FIRE OUTSIDE!
YOUR FEAT AT THE BRIDGE SEEMS FUTILE, HANDSOME ONE! KLANG HOLDS US AS A VISE! ESCAPE IS CUT OFF — AND SURRENDER MEANS TORTURE AND EXECUTION! AMUSING IRONY THAT THE TENDER APRIL BEGGED TO REMAIN WITH THE DRAGON LADY!
TERRY AND I ARE ON KLANG'S BLACK LIST UP TO THE HILT... BUT APRIL AND THE CRISPIN KID SHOULD NOT SUFFER FOR OUR TROUBLES! — HEY, LISTEN!
PLANES!
TAKE COVER!
SLIGHT DAMAGE!
JUST WARMING UP! THEY'LL IMPROVE! THAT SETTLES IT! CRISPIN, HOW'S YOUR NERVE?
STEADY ON, I HOPE, MR. RYAN!

YOU CAN SEE THE DANGER OF OUR SITUATION... IT IS OUR DUTY TO SEE THAT APRIL KANE GETS OUT OF HERE ALIVE... ARE YOU WILLING TO GO OUT TO KLANG WITH A FLAG OF TRUCE — AND INCIDENTALLY, UNDER COVER OF OUR GUNS — AND REQUEST LIBERTY FOR YOU AND THE GIRL? SHE COULDN'T GO ALONE!
I QUITE UNDERSTAND... I AM THEN TO SEE HER SAFELY BACK TO HONGKONG! YES! I WILL DO IT, SIR!
HELLO, THERE! I AM A BRITISH SUBJECT! WILL YOU SEND OUT SOMEONE TO SPEAK WITH ME? I AM COVERED BY RIFLEMEN ON THE CLIFF!
BEHOLD, I, THE GREAT KLANG, COME PERSONALLY TO MAKE SPEECH! NEEDLESS TO SAY, A FALSE MOVE WILL MEAN YOUR DESTRUCTION! NOW, WHAT BRINGS YOU?
THE TWO AMERICANS WHO FOUGHT AGAINST YOU EXPECT NO MERCY AT YOUR HANDS... BUT WITHIN THE BESIEGED VILLAGE IS A YOUNG AMERICAN GIRL...
I COME TO REQUEST THAT YOU ALLOW THIS YOUNG LADY AND ME TO LEAVE IN PEACE! I WILL ESCORT HER TO SAFETY! WE CAN DO YOU NO HARM!
AMERICAN GIRL! AH, YES! KLANG HEARS RUMORS FROM THE WOUNDED PRISONERS OF THIS DELIGHTFUL WHITE ROSEBUD...
KLANG GRANTS THE REQUEST — BUT YOU, AS AN ENGLISHMAN, WILL BE TURNED OVER TO THE INVADER GENERAL FOR TRANSPORTATION TO HONGKONG... THE PRETTY MISS, BEING AMERICAN, KLANG WILL PERSONALLY RETURN TO HER PEOPLE — AFTER THE DRAGON LADY IS DESTROYED!
IF THAT IS YOUR ANSWER — THEN I FEEL I MAY SPEAK FOR THE YOUNG LADY, AS WELL AS MYSELF...
9-10
...WE HOPE YOU MAY JOLLY WELL ROT BEFORE WE EVEN CONSIDER YOUR OUTRAGEOUS OFFER FOR A SINGLE MOMENT! I BID YOU GOOD DAY, SIR!
HA! IT IS FOR KLANG TO LAUGH! THE SOBER BRITISH YOUTH COMES UNDER THE FLAG OF TRUCE FROM THE DRAGON LADY'S CRUMBLING VILLAGE TO REQUEST FAVORS!
9-11
WOULD IT NOT, PERHAPS, BE WISE TO ALLOW THE BRITISH ONE TO EXIT WITH THE SMALL AMERICAN GIRL — AS HE DESIRED!
BAH — YOU ARE THE OLD WOMAN!
Reg. U. S. Pat. Off.: Copyright, 1939, by News Syndicate Co., Inc.
PROBABLY ALL THE OCCUPANTS OF THE BESIEGED TOWN WILL BE BLOWN TO NOTHING... IF SO, NO TRACE WILL BE FOUND! IF, BY CHANCE, THE WHITE BUD LIVES TO FALL INTO KLANG'S HANDS — IT WOULD FURNISH A MOST DIVERTING INTERLUDE!
....SO KLANG WOULDN'T ALLOW YOU TO TAKE THE TENDER ONE TO SAFETY!
NO, MA'M! HE WOULD HAVE SUBJECTED MISS KANE TO UNSPEAKABLE INDIGNITIES! IF YOU WILL PARDON THE EXPRESSION, I WAS SORELY TEMPTED TO BUST HIM ONE ON THE BEAKER!
MILTON CANIFF
THE BOMBERS ASSIGNED KLANG BY THE INVADER DO MUCH DAMAGE TO THE BUILDINGS! IT IS FORTUNATE THAT MY PEOPLE HAVE DUG INTO THE CLIFFS FOR SHELTER!... EVEN SO, EXTINCTION LOOMS EVER NEARER!
9-12
NO USE KIDDING OURSELVES, BEAUTIFUL, WE'RE IN A MEAN PINCH! FOOD AND AMMUNITION GETTING MIGHTY LOW! LUCKY WE HAVE A SPRING FOR WATER!
EVEN IF WE DON'T DARE TAKE A CHANCE OF APRIL KANE'S FALLING INTO KLANG'S HANDS — PERHAPS WE COULD SLIP THE SOLDIERS' WIVES AND KIDS OUT BEFORE THEY STARVE!
MILTON CANIFF
PERHAPS, HANDSOME ONE — BUT YOU FORGET ONE THING... THE CHINESE WOMAN'S MAN IS HER LIFE! IF THE MAN IS DOOMED SHE CONSIDERS IT HIGH HONOR TO SHARE HIS GREATEST ADVENTURE! OF COURSE, TO YOU OF THE "CIVILIZED" WESTERN WORLD, THIS MAY SEEM ODD... OUR WOMEN ARE SIMPLY NOT WELL ENOUGH EDUCATED TO BE SELFISH!
Reg. U. S. Pat. Off.: Copyright, 1939, by News Syndicate Co., Inc.

ALL NIGHT THOSE SHELLS KEEP BURSTIN'! DOESN'T KLANG EVER LET UP? I CAN'T SLEEP!
PAT RYAN SAYS TH' BOMBIN' AN' SHELLIN' IS TO KEEP TH' DRAGON LADY'S MEN ALWAYS ON TH' ALERT—SO THEY'LL WEAR OUT QUICKER! IT SURE NUFF WORKS WITH OL' ME!
9-13
IT'S WHAT HAPPENS IF KLANG'S MOB FINALLY BREAKS IN.... HAVE YOU THOUGHT ABOUT THAT, APRIL?
I RECKON I HAVE— A BIT,.
TH' DRAGON LADY, PAT AND I WON'T HAVE A CHANCE — BUT KLANG WON'T KILL YOU!... PROMISE ME THAT IF THIS PLACE FALLS, YOU WON'T ALLOW KLANG TO TAKE YOU ALIVE!
Reg. U. S. Pat. Off.: Copyright, 1939, by News Syndicate Co., Inc.
THE YOUNG ONE NEED HAVE NO FEAR ON THAT SCORE!
MILTON CANIFF

WHO IS THERE ?
PAT RYAN! YOU SOUND JITTERY, BEAUTIFUL! IT'S STRANGE TO SEE NERVES SHOWING UP IN THE DRAGON LADY! DON'T LET YOUR SENSE OF HUMOR CRACK UP JUST OVER A FEW BOMBS!
9-14
THE HANDSOME ONE JESTS EASILY! IT MEANS LITTLE TO HIM THAT THE DRAGON LADY IS HELPLESS IN THIS ACCURSED TRAP— WHILE THE VERY EARTH CRIES AT THE TREAD OF EACH INVADER BOOT!
I KNOW HOW YOU FEEL! SOME RELATIVES OF MINE THOUGHT THE SAME WAY IN 1776!
NO DOUBT—BUT THAT DOES NOT RELIEVE THE PRESSURE OF THIS SIEGE!
WE'RE TOO FAR OUTNUMBERED TO FIGHT OUR WAY OUT... I THINK WE'RE DUE TO STAGE A LITTLE THEATRICAL PERFORMANCE!
MILTON CANIFF
THEATRICALS? -BAH!
REMEMBER YOUR BLOOD PRESSURE, BEAUTIFUL!... YOUR PEOPLE ARE BORN DEAD PAN ACTORS... I THINK WE CAN CAST ALL OF THEM IN THE LITTLE DRAMA I HAVE IN MIND!
Reg. U. S. Pat. Off.: Copyright, 1939, by News Syndicate Co., Inc.

THE HANDSOME ONE IS TOO SHREWD TO JEST AT THIS DIRE JUNCTURE! WHAT, THEN, IS THIS SCHEME FOR MASS THEATRICALS?
THE ONLY INFORMATION KLANG GETS OF WHAT GOES ON INSIDE THIS ROCKY TOMB IS WHAT HIS PLANE PILOTS SEE ON THEIR BOMBING RAIDS...
9-15
...HAVE YOUR PEOPLE TAKE POSITIONS LIKE DEAD BODIES IN THE STREETS... MORE OF THEM EACH DAY! THE INVADER WON'T WASTE BOMBS IF HE THINKS WE'RE SO DEFEATED WE'VE STOPPED BURYING OUR DEAD!
THEN, FINALLY, THE ENEMY VENTURES INSIDE OUR DESERTED BARRICADE TO TAKE POSSESSION... THE 'DEAD' COME TO LIFE— AND THE PARTY OF OCCUPATION IS NIPPED FROM KLANG'S FORCE LIKE ROTTEN FRUIT FROM THE TREE!!
MILTON CANIFF
AH, MASTER KLANG, THERE WAS GREAT SLACKENING OF FIRE FROM THE CLIFFS AFTER THE LAST BOMBING RAID!
IT IS REGRETTABLE THAT THE DRAGON LADY MAY BE KILLED BEFORE KLANG REACHES HER!... HER BODY TO PRESENT THE INVADER GENERAL ON A LONG SPIKE WOULD BE SO MUCH MORE INTERESTING IF IT WERE ALIVE!
NEXT NIGHT
Reg. U. S. Pat. Off.: Copyright, 1939, by News Syndicate Co., Inc.

IT IS CLEAR THAT OUR PURPOSE NEARS ACCOMPLISHMENT! THE BESIEGED TOWN LIES IN RUINS! ON OUR LAST FLIGHT NOT ONE RIFLE WAS FIRED AT US!
TRY ONCE MORE —TO BE CERTAIN THAT THERE IS NO TRICK! THEN WE ENTER... KLANG GROWS IMPATIENT FOR THE KILL!
9-16
THE PLANES' APPEARANCES GROW MORE INFREQUENT! THE RUSE SHOWS SIGNS OF SUCCESS!
CAN'T TAKE CHANCES... KEEP THE PEOPLE READY TO FLOP DOWN! THAT SHOULDN'T BE DIFFICULT—WITH THEIR STOMACHS PLAYING TAG WITH THEIR SPINES!
AT THIS MOMENT A 'DEAD' MAN ON THE CLIFF FLASHES A SIGNAL....
Reg. U. S. Pat. Off.: Copyright, 1939, by News Syndicate Co., Inc.
MILTON CANIFF

TERRY AND THE PIRATES
by Milton Caniff

Panel 1: MASTER KLANG, FOR MUCH TIME WE BATTER THE VILLAGE OF THE DRAGON LADY WITH BOMB AND SHELL! FOR TWO DAYS THERE HAS BEEN NO REPLY FROM THE GUNS ON THE CLIFF!

Panel 2: AH, SO! AT LONG LAST FAMINE AND STEEL HAVE TAKEN THEIR TOLL... WE SHALL BE CERTAIN WHEN THE INVADER PILOTS RETURN WITH THEIR REPORT!

Panel 3: THE TWO BOMBERS SLOWLY CIRCLE THE BESIEGED TOWN... NOT EVEN A RIFLE SHOT SOUNDS IN THE LITTERED STREETS....

Panel 4: LATER — WHAT, THEN, IS THE CONDITION OF THE ENEMY'S STUPID GARRISON? / AS WE NOTED BEFORE, THERE IS NO SIGN OF LIFE... ONLY BODIES AMONG THE RUINS! IT IS DESOLATION ITSELF!

Panel 5: THEN ADVANCE AND ENTER WITH A DETACHMENT! THIS DENIES KLANG THE PLEASURE OF A MASS EXECUTION — BUT ONE CANNOT HAVE EVERYTHING!

Panel 6: CAUTIOUSLY THE BANDIT FORCE ENTERS THE UNGUARDED GATEWAY....

Panel 8: NOW!

Panel 9: SUDDENLY THE 'BODIES' OF MEN, WOMEN AND CHILDREN COME TO LIFE AND SWARM OVER KLANG'S STARTLED SOLDIERS....

Panel 10: THE ENTRANCE BARRICADE AGAIN BRISTLES WITH GUNS — CUTTING OFF THE BRIGANDS WITHIN THE ROCKY ENCLOSURE FROM KLANG'S MAIN BODY OUTSIDE....

Panel 11: SUCCESS... THE HANDSOME ONE GUESSED WISELY! WE HAVE CUT KLANG'S FORCE BY MANY MEN... / YEAH — BUT THERE'S NOT EVEN A SANDWICH IN THEIR PACKS! AND I'M HUNGRY ENOUGH TO EAT ANYTHING WITH SOME MEAT ON IT!

9-17

WHAT MADNESS IS THIS ?
MASTER... WE ENTERED THE RUINED VILLAGE— BUT, BEHOLD, THE DEAD LITTERING THE STREETS AROSE AT A SIGNAL AND OVERWHELMED US!
9-18
THIS CANNOT BE!
BUT IT IS SO, MASTER... SEE, AGAIN THE BARRICADE BRISTLES WITH BARKING GUNS!
Reg. U. S. Pat. Off.: Copyright, 1939, by News Syndicate Co., Inc.
FOOLS! ALL FOOLS! ON THE BRINK OF SUCCESS KLANG IS FOILED BY AN IDIOT ARMY! BUT THE END IS NOT YET! OPEN FIRE WITH THE BATTERIES! ORDER THE PLANES STOCKED AND READY TO BOMB THAT VILLAGE UNTIL NO FLESH CAN LIVE!
BUT, MASTER, THERE IS A GREAT COMPANY OF OUR OWN MEN IMPRISONED THERE BY THE DRAGON LADY'S ARMY!
OF COURSE! THIS WILL BE A LESSON TO THEM!!
MILTON CANIFF

THE MORALE OF THE MEN HAS BEEN RAISED BY THIS MASS CAPTURE! THE HANDSOME ONE PLANNED WELL!
THAT'S MIGHTY HIGH PRAISE, COMIN' FROM YOU, BEAUTIFUL!
HEAR ME, WHITE MAN! KLANG WILL BLAST THIS PLACE WITH STEEL AND FIRE! HIS RAGE WILL BE ENORMOUS!
9-19
EVEN NOW THE FIRST GUN OF HIS BATTERY ROARS OUT!
HE'S RIGHT! THAT SKUNK DOESN'T HESITATE TO SHELL HIS OWN MEN!
TO THE CAVES BEFORE THE BARRAGE GETS UNDER WAY!
WE'LL HAVE TO SQUEEZE TO GET THE PRISONERS IN TOO!
SQUEEZE, INDEED! LEAVE THE SWINE TIED IN THE OPEN STREET... THEY WILL LEARN HOW IT FEELS TO BE SHELLED BY THEIR OWN COUNTRYMEN!
?
MILTON CANIFF
Reg. U. S. Pat. Off.: Copyright, 1939, by News Syndicate Co., Inc.

THESE MEN ARE PRISONERS OF WAR! YOU CAN'T LEAVE THEM TO DIE LIKE RATS!
CAN'T I? IF THEY TRY TO ENTER OUR SHELTERS I SHALL ORDER MY MEN TO SHOOT THEM DOWN!
9-20
DO AS YOU LIKE! I CAN'T STAND TO HEAR THEM SCREAMING! FOLLOW ME, YOU MUGGS!
Reg. U. S. Pat. Off.: Copyright, 1939, by News Syndicate Co., Inc.
TELL THEM TO LIE CLOSE TO THE ROCK IN A SINGLE LINE! THE EXPLOSIONS GO UP—WE'RE SAFEST FLAT IN THE ANGLE OF ROCK AND EARTH!
THE WHITE GENTLEMAN MAY NOT LISTEN TO THE WORD OF A RENEGADE— BUT I PROMISE THIS KINDNESS WILL NOT BE FORGOTTEN!
AS ONE BUM TO ANOTHER— FORGET IT! AND KEEP YOUR HEAD DOWN—OR YOU WON'T HAVE TO BOTHER!
MILTON CANIFF

MASTER, THE GUNS GROW WHITE HOT! IT IS DANGEROUS TO CONTINUE THE BARRAGE!
THEN CEASE UNTIL THEY COOL! FAH! EVEN THE GUNS FAIL KLANG IN THIS HOUR OF REPRISAL!
9-21
THE POPGUNS HAVE LET UP! DIG YOURSELVES OUT AND COUNT THE BUTCHER BILL... DON'T TRY ANY FUNNY BUSINESS!
Reg. U. S. Pat. Off.: Copyright, 1939, by News Syndicate Co., Inc.
DEETH! -TERRY AND APRIL OKAY?
YES, MR. RYAN! THE SHELTER IN THE ROCKS YOU DUG FOR US SERVED VERY NICELY!
GOOD! HELLO, BEAUTIFUL! THAT LAST ONE WAS PRETTY TOUGH... SORRY I HAD TO CROSS YOU ON LEAVING THOSE PRISONERS TO DIE!
MILTON CANIFF

HEY, MAMA, WHY THE BIG FREEZE? SURELY YOU'RE NOT SORE BECAUSE I DIDN'T WANT THOSE PRISONERS TO DIE LIKE VERMIN... EVEN IF THEY ARE!
AFTER ALL, THEY'RE HELPLESS... AND PRISONERS OF WAR AT THAT! EVEN THE BARBARIAN TRIBES RESPECTED THAT RULE OF CONFLICT!
WE'VE MADE A BIG DENT IN KLANG'S FORCE —THAT SHOULD BE ENOUGH TO SERVE THE PURPOSE! NOW WE CAN COOK UP ANOTHER TRICK TO CONFUSE HIM FURTHER!
MILTON CANIFF
Reg. U. S. Pat. Off.; Copyright, 1939, by News Syndicate Co., Inc.
SERVE THE USUAL MEAGRE RATIONS TO MY MEN—BUT NONE TO THE PRISONERS! THEY SHALL KNOW HOW IT FEELS TO STARVE WHILE THEIR MASTER KLANG SPICES THEIR HUNGER WITH IRON FROM TIME TO TIME!
9-22

HEY, LISTEN, BABE, I CAN STAND A LOT— BUT NOT SEEING MEN DELIBERATELY STARVED... WHILE THERE'S STILL SOME GRUB AROUND!
THE DRAGON LADY IS NOT A BABE — AND IT MATTERS NOT WHAT YOU CAN STAND!
...SUCH A TENDER HEARTED ONE DESERVES NO EXPLANATION... BUT LET IT SUFFICE THAT THESE MEN SHALL NOT HAVE ONE BITE OF THE PRECIOUS FOOD ON WHICH MY MEN MUST EXIST!
DON'T GIVE ME THAT TENDER STUFF! YOU KNOW I'M NO PANTY WAIST... BUT EVEN A BUNCH OF KLANG'S PUNKS DESERVE HUMANE TREATMENT—WHEN THEY'RE HELPLESS!
MILTON CANIFF
Reg. U. S. Pat. Off.; Copyright, 1939, by News Syndicate Co., Inc.
SINCE YOU FEEL SO GENEROUSLY DISPOSED TOWARD THOSE SWINE... I SHALL HAVE YOUR PORTION DIVIDED AMONG THEM... IT WILL GIVE EACH MAN ABOUT ONE GRAIN OF RICE AT EACH MEAL!
9-23

TERRY AND THE PIRATES
by MILTON CANIFF
Reg. U. S. Pat. Off.; Copyright, 1939, by News Syndicate Co., Inc.
HO, KLANG'S LAST BOMBARDMENT AS REPRISAL FOR THE PRISONERS WE TOOK WAS THE WORST SO FAR!
ALAS, THERE ARE GREATER PROBLEMS! THE MASTER AND THE WHITE GIANT DISAGREE OVER THE TREATMENT OF THE PRISONERS!
LISTEN, BEAUTIFUL, YOU KNOW THE RULES OF WAR; AS THEY ARE LAUGHINGLY CALLED, AS WELL AS I! WE HAVE LITTLE ENOUGH TO EAT— BUT WE STILL DON'T HAVE TO LET THESE PRISONERS STARVE!
THE DRAGON LADY HAS SPOKEN! NOT ONE MORSEL OF OUR PITIFUL RATIONS DO THE DOGS GET!
WE ARE DOOMED! MASTER KLANG SHELLS THIS PLACE—CARING NOT IF WE, TOO, ARE SLAIN! NOW WE STARVE! IT WAS BETTER ON MY POOR, BARREN LAND IN THE NORTH!
WHINING WILL NOT HELP, FOOL! THE WHITE MAN PLEADS FOR US... PERHAPS EVEN YET HE WILL SAVE US —ALTHOUGH I KNOW NOT WHY! STRANGE, THESE WESTERN PEOPLES!
COME ON, HONEY CHILE; ACT YOUR AGE — THESE AREN'T CAVE-MAN TIMES! GIVE THOSE POOR DEVILS THE JUSTICE DUE ANY PRISONER OF WAR!
THE DRAGON LADY NEED NOT LISTEN TO THESE WORDS OF OCCIDENTAL SOFT HEARTEDNESS! INDEED, SHE WILL NOT!
THE PROBLEM SHALL BE SOLVED COMPLETELY! LINE THOSE PRISONERS UP AND SHOOT THEM!

HEY!
NO FURTHER WORDS ARE NECESSARY! DO NOT FORCE ME TO INCLUDE YOU, HANDSOME ONE!
THREE AT A TIME WILL SUFFICE! READY! AIM! FIRE! ...I SAID, FIRE!!
MASTER, FORGIVE US...
FORGIVE YOU? GET INTO LINE AND DIRECT YOUR SQUAD TO FIRE BEFORE I RIDDLE YOUR BONES!
YOU MAY STRIKE ME DOWN, MASTER—BUT THE MEN FEEL AS I DO! YOU WELL KNOW WE WOULD FOLLOW YOU TO CERTAIN DEATH AGAINST THE ARMED ENEMIES OF CHINA...
...BUT WE WERE SIMPLE FARMERS BEFORE THIS WAR—AND WILL BE AGAIN, IF WE LIVE! THE PRISONERS BEFORE US ARE LIKE OURSELVES—MISGUIDED THOUGH THEY MAY HAVE BEEN UNDER KLANG! WHEN THEY BORE ARMS WE COULD FIGHT THEM... BUT AS HELPLESS HUMANS WE CANNOT SHOOT THEM DOWN!
MY WORD! OH, MY WORD, INDEED! DID YOU HEAR WHAT TOOK PLACE?
I KNEW PAT AND TH' DRAGON LADY WERE FUSSIN' BECAUSE SHE DIDN'T WANT TO FEED TH' PRISONERS!
9-25
Reg. U. S. Pat. Off.; Copyright, 1939, by News Syndicate Co., Inc.
OH, BUT THEN SHE BECAME ANGRY AND ORDERED THE POOR WRETCHES SHOT...TO BE RID OF THEM! BUT THE FIRING SQUAD REFUSED TO DO IT!...
...SAID THE PRISONERS WERE JUST POOR FARMERS, LIKE THEMSELVES WHEN NOT BEARING ARMS UNDER KLANG!
LATER
HEY, BEAUTIFUL! STILL PEEVED AT YOUR OLD PAL, PAT?
GO BACK WITH THE OTHER SHEEP-HEARTED WHITE FOOLS...OR I WILL BLOW THE SMIRK FROM YOUR DESPISED FACE!
MILTON CANIFF
EASE OFF THE ARTILLERY, BEAUTIFUL! IF YOU SHOT ME YOU'D BE FRESH OUT OF SOMEONE TO BE ANGRY WITH!
GET OUT!
9-26
I THINK BEING SO HIGH-MINDED AND PATRIOTIC CRAMPS YOUR TECHNIQUE! WHEN YOU WERE A FREE-LANCE HOODLUM YOUR STYLE OF EVIL WAS MUCH MORE SPECTACULAR!
I WISH TO BE ALONE!
Reg. U. S. Pat. Off.; Copyright, 1939, by News Syndicate Co., Inc.
THAT'S ANOTHER THING! YOU'VE BEEN KIDDING YOURSELF THAT YOU'RE A SORT OF FEMALE NAPOLEON! ...YOU HAVE ALL THE TRICKS, BUT WOMEN ARE ALWAYS FAILURES AT SUCH TACTICS! —THEY CAN GO SO FAR—THEN SENTIMENT CATCHES UP WITH THEM—AND THEY THROW A TIRE!
SENTIMENT, BAH!
I THOUGHT YOU'D SCOFF IT OFF...THE THING THAT'S EATING YOU IS THAT YOU'RE SMART ENOUGH TO KNOW YOU'RE A SOFTY AT HEART—BUT YOUR DESIRE TO BE A TOUGH GUY MAKES YOU AFRAID TO SHOW IT! SIT DOWN AND LET'S TALK IT OVER—WE'VE SEEN ALL THE MOVIES IN TOWN, ANYHOW!
MILTON CANIFF

FUNNY HOW WOMEN CAN BE REALISTIC ABOUT EVERYTHING BUT THEMSELVES! THEY KNOW THEY CAN RULE AN EMPIRE—BUT IN THE FINAL PAY-OFF THEY AREN'T SATISFIED UNLESS SOMEONE RULES THEM!
NO PERSON RULES THE DRAGON LADY!
SURE... THAT'S WHAT CLEOPATRA AND QUEEN ELIZABETH THOUGHT—BUT THEY BOTH REALIZED, FINALLY, THERE WAS NO USE KIDDING THEMSELVES—THAT A WOMAN CAN'T BE REALLY SATISFIED WITH ABSOLUTE POWER! IT'S HER DESTINY TO BE CONQUERED!
THEN WHAT, MY ANALYTICAL ONE, DO YOU SUGGEST THE DRAGON LADY SHOULD DO ABOUT IT?
... IT'S NOT MY PROBLEM! I'M JUST TELLING YOU... IF YOU DON'T RECOGNIZE THE WEAKNESS IN YOUR ARMOR, IT WILL BE YOUR DOWNFALL!
THE DRAGON LADY DOES RECOGNIZE HER WEAKNESS... IT IS IN ALLOWING YOUR PRESENCE HERE TO LOWER FOR A MOMENT THE IRON MASK OF HER RESERVE! ...THAT PRESENCE MUST BE ELIMINATED!
9-27
Reg. U. S. Pat. Off.; Copyright, 1939, by News Syndicate Co., Inc.
MILTON CANIFF

A SHOT!
FROM THE DRAGON LADY'S QUARTERS! SHOULD WE MAKE HASTE TO THE SPOT?
IF WE VALUE OUR LIVES—NO! IN HER PRESENT ANGER AT OUR REFUSAL TO MURDER THE PRISONERS HER IRE WOULD VENT ITSELF ON US! LET THE FATES WEAVE THEIR OWN PATTERN!
WHY DID YOU MISS?
AT A RANGE OF FOUR FEET YOU MISSED BECAUSE YOU WANTED TO! YOU HAD TO JUSTIFY THE NAPOLEON INSTINCT!...
... NOW IT'S DONE, AND YOU CAN ADMIT THAT YOU'RE JUST A WOMAN!! COME HERE!
9-28
Reg. U. S. Pat. Off.; Copyright, 1939, by News Syndicate Co., Inc.
MILTON CANIFF

YOU'VE BEEN WAGING A BATTLE BETWEEN YOUR SENSE AND YOUR SENSES ... THE SENSES ARE WINNING — AND YOU'RE GLAD - BECAUSE YOU WEARY OF THE STRIFE ...
... NOW THE BLOOD RED OF YOUR LIPS GROWS DEEPER WITH THE LUXURY OF ABANDON .... BUT YOUR EYES STILL SMOLDER WITH THE FIRE OF SELF-TYRANNY .... PERHAPS YOU NEED SOME HELP IN MAKING UP YOUR MIND....
9-29
MILTON CANIFF
Reg. U. S. Pat. Off.; Copyright, 1939, by News Syndicate Co., Inc.

MASTER KLANG, THE MESSENGER FROM THE INVADER GENERAL SAID THERE IS GREAT IMPATIENCE THAT THE DRAGON LADY IS NOT YET A PRISONER!
SO!... TONIGHT, AS THE LONE MACHINE GUNNER GUARDS THAT NARROW, REMOTE PASS INTO THE BESIEGED VILLAGE, WE WILL ACCOMPLISH WHAT BOMBS AND SHELLS HAVE FAILED TO DO!
IS ALL IN READINESS?
AYE, MASTER! THE DELECTABLE STEW SIMMERS IN THE VESSEL—AND THE NIGHT WIND BLOWS TOWARD THE SENTINEL IN THE PASS!
THEN PROCEED!
9-30
Reg. U. S. Pat. Off., Copyright, 1939, by News Syndicate Co., Inc.
MILTON CANIFF

TERRY AND THE PIRATES
by MILTON CANIFF
I'M NOT HUNGRY, APRIL!
HUSH UP! YOU'RE TRYIN' T' SKIMP SO I'LL HAVE MORE TO EAT... BUT YOU'RE THE ONE WHO NEEDS NOURISHIN' MOST, MR. TERRY LEE!
IT'S DIFFICULT FOR LEE TO GAIN HIS STRENGTH BACK WITH SO LITTLE FOOD! ... HOW DO YOU FEEL, APRIL?
SORTA BOILED DOWN... IT'S THOSE AWFUL SHELLS BOOMIN' THAT FRETS ME MOST, THOUGH! I'M IN A KIND OF DAZE!
OH, DEETH, I HATE BEIN' A SISSY.... BUT I'M 'BOUT READY TO DROP! EVEN THOUGH PAT RYAN AN' TH' DRAGON LADY HAVE PATCHED UP THEIR FUSS I'VE 'BOUT GIVEN UP HOPE!
... I SAY, THAT WON'T DO, YOU KNOW! THEY'LL SEE US THROUGH, I'M SURE... I ONLY WISH THAT I MIGHT COME FORWARD WITH SOME MAGNIFICENT GESTURE, BUT I AM NOT THE ... AH... HEROIC TYPE!
JUST BEYOND THE GUERILLAS' SENTRY POST IN A PASS THROUGH THE NATURAL ROCK WALLS OF THE BESIEGED VILLAGE ....
THEY PRESUME TO OUTWIT THE GREAT KLANG, BUT THEY KNOW NOT THE EXTENT OF MY CLEVERNESS!
AGAIN THE WIND BLOWS TOWARD YONDER SENTRY, MASTER!
.... NIGHT AFTER NIGHT AS THIS UNWORTHY ONE STANDS GUARD, SICK WITH HUNGER AND WORRY FOR MY WIFE AND CHILD, THE DEVILS BEYOND THE ROCKS PREPARE GREAT FEASTS OF FINE MEAT AND RICE!
THE PREVAILING WIND CARRIES THE MADDENING ODOR TO THESE NOSTRILS — SO LONG UNTOUCHED BY THE FRAGRANCE OF ANY COOKED FOOD! THE MIND REFLECTS THAT OUR CAUSE IS A RIGHTEOUS ONE... BUT THE REALISTIC STOMACH TAKES NOTE THAT THE FORCES OF EVIL DINE MOST WELL!
HALLOO, WATCHFUL ONE! WHY BE THE FOOLISH SLAVE OF INEVITABLE DESTRUCTION? ALLOW OUR COLUMNS TO PASS YOUR STAND WITHOUT GIVING THE ALARM AND THIS FINE FEAST IS THEN YOURS, ALL YOURS! ENOUGH FOR YOUR FAMILY AS WELL — IF SUCH YOU POSSESS!
MY WIFE AND INFANT SON SLEEP BENEATH YONDER CRAG! WE COULD TAKE THE FOOD AND ESCAPE TO THE HILLS! NONE WOULD KNOW OF MY TREACHERY IN THE CONFUSION THAT WILL FOLLOW! FORGIVE ME, MASTER DRAGON LADY, I DO THIS THAT MY SON MAY LIVE!
YES, YOU MAY PASS!
ON SILENT FEET THE MEN OF KLANG SLIP THROUGH THE NARROW OPENING ... A DARK SNAKE WITH FANGS OF STEEL ....
WHEN DO I RECEIVE THE REWARD? THE FOOD? WHERE IS THE FEAST?
AH, THE FOOD! ...THERE WAS NOT TIME TO BRING IT...
... BUT THAT SHOULD SATISFY A TRAITOR'S APPETITE .... HAHAHAHA!!

HAH, THE STUPID PEASANT— AS ALWAYS, A SLAVE TO HIS STOMACH! HE BETRAYS HIS TRUST FOR THE PROMISE OF A MEAL! KLANG'S STEEL WILL SILENCE HIS HUNGER—AND ANY POSSIBLE ALARM!
10-2
THE PLEASURE OF THIS MOMENT IS INTOLERABLE! THE DRAGON LADY'S VILLAGE LIES HELPLESS AT KLANG'S FEET... CIRCLE THE PLACE AND ATTACK AT THE SIGNAL...
DEETH, HONEY, MY KNEES ARE JUS' TAPPIN' AWAY FROM WEAKNESS! I'M SO HUNGRY I'M LIGHT-HEADED ALL OVER!
WAIT HERE, APRIL, I'LL FETCH HALF OF OUR TOMORROW'S RATION OF RICE... WE'LL HAVE A FEAST!
MILTON CANIFF
Reg. U. S. Pat. Off.; Copyright, 1939, by News Syndicate Co., Inc.

WISH DEETH WOULD HURRY! I'M NOT ONLY HUNGRY —BUT LONE---
YEEEEEE!!
10-3
Reg. U. S. Pat. Off.; Copyright, 1939, by News Syndicate Co., Inc.
CURSE THAT LITTLE FOOL! SILENCE HER!
KLANG FIRES THREE QUICK SHOTS... THE SIGNAL TO ATTACK!
OH, MY WORD... I SAY... GOOD HEAVENS... WHAT DOES ONE DO?
MILTON CANIFF

10-4
Reg. U. S. Pat. Off.; Copyright, 1939, by News Syndicate Co., Inc.
WH...
IT'S A RAID! SHOOT YOUR WAY OUT, BEAUTIFUL!
BEING NO FOOL, THE DRAGON LADY WILL NOT HEED THE SHOUTED WORDS OF ADVICE!
MILTON CANIFF

I SAY, THEY'VE MISSED ME — AND THE PASS THEY ENTERED STANDS UNGUARDED ...MR. RYAN WOULD MAKE A DASH TO THE INVADER GENERAL TO SEEK MERCY FOR US NEUTRALS... MY COURSE IS CLEAR — IF I HAVE THE STRENGTH
10-5
Reg. U. S. Pat. Off.; Copyright, 1939, by News Syndicate Co., Inc.
AT THIS MOMENT THE PRISONERS HELD BY THE DRAGON LADY ARE RELEASED BY KLANG'S EXULTING TROOPS....
COME QUICKLY TO MASTER KLANG!
AYE!
BEHOLD! DOES ONE OF THE DOGS ATTEMPT ESCAPE THROUGH YONDER RAVINE?
MILTON CANIFF

HO! YOUR EYES PLAY TRICKS! I SEE NO FUGITIVE RUNNING AWAY THROUGH THE RAVINE!
OOOOH!
10-6
Reg. U. S. Pat. Off.: Copyright, 1939, by News Syndicate Co., Inc.
GO, SLIGHT ONE... CARRY YOUR PLEA FOR MERCY TO THE INVADER GENERAL! LET THIS BE SOME SMALL COMPENSATION FOR THE KINDNESS OF THE WHITE GIANT WHO SAVED OUR LIVES IN THE BOMBARDMENT!
THE DOGS ARE SUBDUED, MASTER! THE DRAGON LADY'S TROOPS INFLICTED BUT THREE CASUALTIES!
THEN WHY THIS MASS OF MOANING WRETCHES?
...WHY...AH...THOSE ARE THE MEN WHO SUBDUED THE WHITE MAN!
MILTON CANIFF

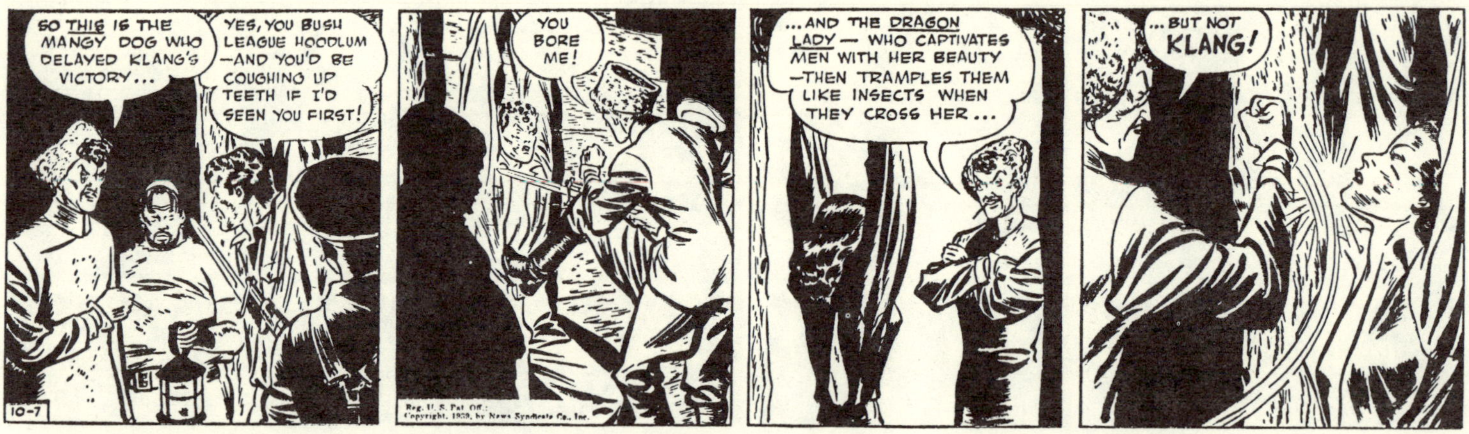
SO THIS IS THE MANGY DOG WHO DELAYED KLANG'S VICTORY...
YES, YOU BUSH LEAGUE HOODLUM —AND YOU'D BE COUGHING UP TEETH IF I'D SEEN YOU FIRST!
10-7
YOU BORE ME!
Reg. U. S. Pat. Off.: Copyright, 1939, by News Syndicate Co., Inc.
...AND THE DRAGON LADY — WHO CAPTIVATES MEN WITH HER BEAUTY —THEN TRAMPLES THEM LIKE INSECTS WHEN THEY CROSS HER...
...BUT NOT KLANG!

TERRY
MILTON CANIFF
KLANG'S TROOPS STEAL QUIETLY INTO THE DRAGON LADY'S VILLAGE .... WHEN THE RUSE IS DISCOVERED THERE IS A SHORT, SHARP FIGHT —BUT THE SURPRISE IS COMPLETE — AND KLANG RULES SUPREME!
AH, SUCH EXQUISITE PLEASURE! THAT RAGING ONE ANNOYED US AT THE BRIDGE... I THINK IT WOULD BE AMUSING TO DRAG HIM THROUGH BROKEN GLASS — THEN HANG HIM BY THE EARS!
... AND KLANG'S HIGHLY RESPECTED ANTAGONIST, THE LADY OF THE DRAGONS! HAHAHA! YOU, MY TREASURE, WILL HAVE THE SKIN CUT FROM YOUR TOO BEAUTIFUL FACE — THEN MY MEN WILL CARRY YOU TO THE INVADER GENERAL ON THE POINTS OF THEIR BAYONETS — AS PROOF OF KLANG'S VICTORY!
THE FAIR ONE APPEARS WEAKENED BY THE ORDEAL OF THE SIEGE... I THINK WE WILL CUT OFF HIS ARM AND FEED IT TO HIM — TO BRING HIS STRENGTH BACK!
THIS, THEN, IS THE SOFT LITTLE PETAL THE YOUNG ENGLISHMAN WISHED TO ESCORT TO HONGKONG! THERE WILL, OF COURSE, BE NO TORTURE FOR SUCH AN INNOCENT ONE! KLANG HONORS HER WITH THE PRIVILEGE OF HELPING HIM SPEND THE INVADER GOLD TO BE PAID FOR THE CAPTURE OF THE DRAGON LADY! HAHAHAHA!

...BUT WHERE IS THE HIGH-MINDED BRITISH LAD? I HAD PLANS FOR HIM!
ALAS, MASTER, HE PROBABLY DIED IN THE FIGHTING... HE IS NOWHERE ABOUT! OBVIOUSLY A WEAK PERSON... HE WOULD HAVE EXPIRED TOO QUICKLY UNDER TORTURE — VERY BORING!
...THAT FAT CHAP IN THE RED SHIRT... ALLOWED ME TO SLIP AWAY... MUST HAVE BEEN GRATITUDE FOR MR. RYAN SAVING HIS LIFE! ...MUST GET TO THE INVADER CAMP... FOLLOW THIS ROAD KLANG'S MEN CAME ON... INVADER GENERAL WOULDN'T ALLOW NEUTRALS TO BE TORTURED... MUST SAVE MY FRIENDS.... MUST!
IS FUME! IS FURY! ...'CAUSE MIST' PAT SLIP AWAY, OL' INVLADER GENERAL PUT WE IN HOOSYGOW! BIG STOOPER START TO BOUNCE GUARD ON CEILING — BUT CONNIE STOP SAME 'CAUSE MIST' PAT SAY NO DO NAUGHTIES!

NO NEWSIES COME... WE NOT KNOW WHERE MIST' PAT, MIST' TERRY, MISSY APLIL, MIST' DEET' CLISPIN — OR OL' DLAGON LADY! IS MUSS! IS MAD! IS MESS.... OH! OH!
10-8
...FOR DAYS AFTER DAYS CONNIE'S EARS TWITCH... NOW THEY FLIP-FLAP LIKE WINGS! ...IS CERTAIN SIGN THAT FLIENDS IN TLOUBLE — BIG TLOUBLE! OH, WOE!

...IS MIST' DEET CLISPIN NUMBER TREE! CONNIE KNOW FACE FLOM PICTURE IN NEWSYPAPER! HIM ACT SECRET... LIKE AFLAID OF GUARDS! CONNIE MOTION HIM TO GO UP TOP-SIDE ROOF! STOOPER POOF OUT LIGHT AN' DO LIKE CONNIE SAY!
10-9
DO!
CRASH! FROM THE PRISON HUT!
BEST TO INVESTIGATE!
...HOW MANY TIMES CONNIE SAY NOT TO WALK IN SLEEP AN' MAKE STUMBLES WITH HUGE-ISH FOOTS?
MILTON CANIFF
Reg. U. S. Pat. Off.; Copyright, 1939, by News Syndicate Co., Inc.

MIST' DEET' CLISPIN NUMBER TREE! WE KNOW YOU FLOM PICTURE! ME CONNIE — THIS BIG STOOPER... HUMBLE AT SERVICE! WHERE FLIENDS?
ALL AT THE DRAGON LADY'S VILLAGE... KLANG CAPTURED IT — I ALONE ESCAPED! I TRIED TO GET THE INVADER GENERAL TO SAVE THE WHITE PEOPLE — HIS AIDES WOULDN'T ALLOW ME INSIDE HIS QUARTERS! MR. RYAN DESCRIBED YOU TWO — SAID YOU'D PROBABLY BE IMPRISONED HERE!
10-10
CONNIE THINKIN' LIKE FEVERISH! SEE CHUG-BUGGIES IN BIG PARKIN' PLACE? WE GONNA BORROW COUPLE OF SAME!
...YOU MEAN TO DRIVE TO HELP THEM, I SUPPOSE! BUT HOW CAN WE FACE KLANG'S ENTIRE ARMY?
Reg. U. S. Pat. Off.; Copyright, 1939, by News Syndicate Co., Inc.
WE CROSS THAT BRIDGE WHEN WELL RUNS DRY! NOW-TIME YOU KETCHUM BIG GAS-WAGON WHILE STOOPER AN' CONNIE MAKE DISTRACTIONS FOR GUARDS!
I CAN PROBABLY GET AWAY — BUT WHAT ABOUT YOU TWO?
IF WE SUCCEEDFUL, WE KETCHUM BUS, ALSO! ...IF NO LUCKY — WELL, HAS BEEN MOST NICE TO HAVE KNOW SUCH FINE YOUNG GENTLEMANS LIKE YOU ARE SAME! NOW GO PLEASE — OF A SUDDEN!
MILTON CANIFF

DEETH CRAWLS ALONG THE LINE OF INVADER CARS UNTIL HE FINDS ONE THAT GIVES OFF HEAT... HE SLIPS BEHIND THE WHEEL, KNOWING THE MOTOR WILL TURN OVER EASILY....

IGNITION KEY STILL IN... LUCK! IF THERE'S ONLY PLENTY OF PETROL!

10-11

HAYAH! THIEVES!

WHAT IS?

THIS IS!

WELL, BEAUTIFUL, LOOKS AS IF SOMEBODY DEALT US THE JOKER THIS TIME!

WHEN ONE RIDES THE TIGER, HE MUST EXPECT A VIOLENT END TO THE JOURNEY!

THE CHINESE BELIEVES THAT TO JOIN ONE'S ANCESTORS IS THE GREATEST OF ALL GLORIES —AND TAKES COMFORT FROM THE THOUGHT!

BABY, IF YOUR ANCESTORS WERE ANYTHING LIKE YOU, I'LL BET IT'D BE A LOT LESS VIOLENT TO KEEP RIGHT ON BATTLING THE TIGER!

10-12

THE INNOCENT ONE CRINGES IN FEAR BEFORE THE GREAT KLANG! THAT IS CHARMING! COME, KLANG DOES NOT INTEND TO TORTURE SO SOFT A PETAL!

I HATE YOU, YOU AWFUL OL' THING! MR. RYAN WOULD FIX YOU IF HE WERE FREE!

...BUT THE ESTEEMED ONE IS NOT FREE! KLANG ADMIRES THE SPIRIT OF THE SAUCY ONE, HOWEVER, AND WILL ALLOW HER TO DINE AT HIS FEET!

ARE...ARE MY FRIENDS BEING FED TOO?

THOSE PIGS? BUT OF COURSE NOT! WHY SHOULD KLANG WASTE FOOD ON NEAR-CORPSES?

THEN I SHALL NOT TOUCH A BITE OF YOUR EVIL OL' DINNER!

SUCH TOUCHING LOYALTY! IT IS UNFORTUNATE! KLANG HAD HIS CHEF PREPARE FRIED CHICKEN, BEATEN BISCUITS AND SWEET POTATO PIE IN HONOR OF THE OCCASION!

OOOOHH! AND YOU SAID YOU WEREN'T GOING TO TORTURE ME !!!

10-13

THE INNOCENT ONE AMUSES KLANG— BUT THERE ARE MORE IMPORTANT MATTERS AT HAND! TAKE HER AWAY!

DAWN IS NEAR! LINE UP THE ENTIRE SURVIVING POPULATION OF THE DRAGON LADY'S VILLAGE IN THE FLAT VALLEY OUTSIDE THE ROCKY ENCLOSURE! MY ARMY WILL THEN EXECUTE THEM IN ONE VOLLEY! THE DRAGON LADY AND THE WHITE MEN WE WILL TORTURE AT LEISURE AFTERWARD!

WE MOST LUCKY —BUT MUS' WORK FASTISH BEFORE INVADERS COME CLIPPITY-BANG! WHERE CAN BEST GO SEE DLAGON LADY'S VILLAGE?

UP ON THOSE ROCKS— IF I CAN MAKE IT... I'M SO WEAK FROM HUNGER!

OH, MY WORD! WHAT CAN WE DO? THEY SEEM TO BE PREPARING TO SHOOT THE DRAGON LADY'S PEOPLE DOWN ENMASSE!

IS AWFULS ... BUT WAIT! CONNIE GOT BLAIN-BUMPS! QUICK! TO GASSY WAGONS! IS LONG CHANCE — BUT NO CHANCE, NO CHIPS! COME IMMEDIATE!

10-14

TERRY AND THE PIRATES
by Milton Caniff
Reg. U. S. Pat. Off., Copyright, 1939, by News Syndicate Co., Inc.
UNABLE TO MAKE HIS PLEA TO THE INVADER GENERAL, DEETH CRISPIN HELPS CONNIE AND BIG STOOP ESCAPE... THE THREE GET AWAY IN TWO INVADER CARS AND RACE TO THE SURRENDERED VILLAGE..
THAT MADMAN, KLANG, IS LINING UP THOSE POOR PEOPLE FOR A MASS EXECUTION!
IS SO! -US GET MOVIN'!
BUT WHAT CAN WE DO? THREE AGAINST AN ARMY? AND I ABOUT TO FLINK OUT FROM HUNGER?
PLEASE TO NOT DO SO FOR LITTLE TIME, MIST' DEET CLISPIN NUMBER TREE! CONNIE GOT PLAN – CLAZY AS COOTIE-BUG – BUT NO TIME FOR SENSIBLES! GIVE LISTENS, PLEASE...
HA-HO! SEE THE PIGS CRINGE! KLANG'S ARMY WILL RID THE EARTH OF THEM — ALL IN ONE MAGNIFICENT VOLLEY! THE LONG SINGLE LINE WILL MAKE IT MORE SPECTACULAR!
KLANG BRINGS THE ESTEEMED ONES TO WITNESS THE GRAND PURGE! THE CLIMAX WILL BE YOUR TORTURE!
GEE, PAT...
STEADY, PAL, ...GAME'S NOT OVER 'TIL THE WHISTLE BLOWS! GLAD HE LEFT APRIL OUT OF THIS!
THERE IS LITTLE TIME REMAINING... LET THE HANDSOME ONE KNOW THAT THE DRAGON LADY HAS FOUND HIS COMPANY A PLEASANT LAST MEMORY!
THANKS, BEAUTIFUL! YOU'RE STRICTLY FRONT ROW CENTER YOURSELF! IF A GUY HAS TO GO OUT IT'S NICE TO DO IT WITH HIS SENSES REELING!
READY! AIM...
HOLD, MASTER! DO I NOT SEE. THE OFFICIAL AUTOMOBILES OF THE INVADER GENERAL ENTERING THE VALLEY?
INDEED! WHAT GOOD FORTUNE! THE GENERAL SHALL WITNESS IN PERSON THE RESULT OF KLANG'S GOOD WORK! ATTENTION! EYES FRONT!
IS NOW-TIME!
10-15

KLANG SEES TWO OFFICIAL INVADER CARS COMING INTO THE VALLEY JUST AS THE EXECUTION IS TO BEGIN..... BELIEVING THEY CONTAIN THE INVADER GENERAL AND HIS STAFF, HE CALLS HIS MEN TO ATTENTION... THEN —
10-16
Reg. U. S. Pat. Off.: Copyright, 1939, by News Syndicate Co., Inc.
YEE-OW TOUCHDOWN!
MILTON CANIFF

HO, MIST' PAT! US COME CLIPPITY BOOM-BANG! CUT LAWN SLICK! PLETTY SMART, YOU BETME!
YOU DID, AND YOU ARE! CUT US DOWN BEFORE THOSE GUYS OF KLANG'S GET SOBER!
QUICKLY, WE MUST FREE MY PEOPLE SO THEY MAY TAKE UP THE ENEMY'S WEAPONS!
10-17
IS FACT, MISSY DLAGON LADY! OL' INVADER COME PLENTY CHOP-CHOP! —US BORROW GAS-BUGGIES!
GATHER GUNS AND FOOD FROM THE FALLEN! SCATTER TO THE HILLS... I WILL JOIN YOU AT SOWUNG TEMPLE! GO!
MR. RYAN! THERE GOES KLANG! HE HID IN THOSE ROCKS IN THE CONFUSION! WE MUST PUNISH HIM!
MILTON CANIFF
Reg. U. S. Pat. Off.: Copyright, 1939, by News Syndicate Co., Inc.

DEETH!... HEY, TERRY! CONNIE! THE KID'S HIT!
OH, MY WORD!
10-18
Reg. U. S. Pat. Off.: Copyright, 1939, by News Syndicate Co., Inc.
MAKE A COMPRESS! THAT SKUNK USED DUM-DUM BULLETS! YOU'LL BE OKAY, FELLAH!
YOU'RE... MOST... COMFORTING, MR. RYAN— BUT I FEEL A BIT GONE INSIDE...
MILTON CANIFF
PAT! KLANG PROBABLY LEFT APRIL BACK IN THE VILLAGE— ...HE RAN THAT WAY!
TAKE CARE OF CRISPIN! KLANG AND I ARE GOING TO KEEP A LITTLE DATE!
I SAY, LEE! ..WOULD YOU MIND NOT TELLING MISS KANE THAT I RATHER BOTCHED THINGS AT THE END? —I WANTED SO BADLY TO BRING IT OFF WELL— BUT I GUESS I'M... JUST... NOT THE... HERO TYPE!

WHAT EVIL FATE PURSUES KLANG WHEN HE ENCOUNTERS THOSE AMERICAN SWINE? BUT DISASTER TO ME WILL COST THEM ONE THING!
10-19
MILTON CANIFF
WHAT HAPPENED? DID YOU HURT MY FRIENDS, YOU HORRIBLE OL' THING?
AT LEAST THIS WHITE FLESH SHALL BREAK AT THE HAND OF KLANG! OPEN YOUR MOUTH!!
THAT'S JUST TO EVEN THINGS UP, SADIE! NOW WE'LL CANCEL THE ARTILLERY AND I'LL DO A LITTLE FLESH-BREAKING THAT WILL LAST!
Reg. U. S. Pat. Off.: Copyright, 1939, by News Syndicate Co., Inc.

COME, YOUNG ONE, THERE IS LITTLE TIME FOR EMOTION—EVEN THOUGH THE HEART IS FULL! THE INVADER PACK WILL BE IN FULL CRY!
I KNOW!
10-20
IN THE TWO CARS WE CAN REACH THE RIVER —THERE WILL BE BRITISH AND AMERICAN SHIPS OF SOME SORT, IN SPITE OF THE WAR!
BUT PAT! —AND APRIL!
THEY WILL BE ALONG IN A MOMENT.... MEANWHILE--- WHY DOES THAT HUGE CHINESE STARE AT THE DRAGON LADY SO?
Reg. U. S. Pat. Off.; Copyright, 1939, by News Syndicate Co., Inc.
MILTON CANIFF

WHY DOES THAT GREAT OAF GLARE AT ME? WHO IS HE?
THAT'S RIGHT, YOU NEVER SAW HIM BEFORE! WHY, HE'S OUR ...
10-21
Reg. U. S. Pat. Off. Copyright, 1939, by News Syndicate Co., Inc.
I KNOW HIM, NOW! HE WAS MY SERVANT WHEN I WAS A CHILD! IT WAS I WHO ORDERED HIS TONGUE CUT OUT!!
MILTON CANIFF

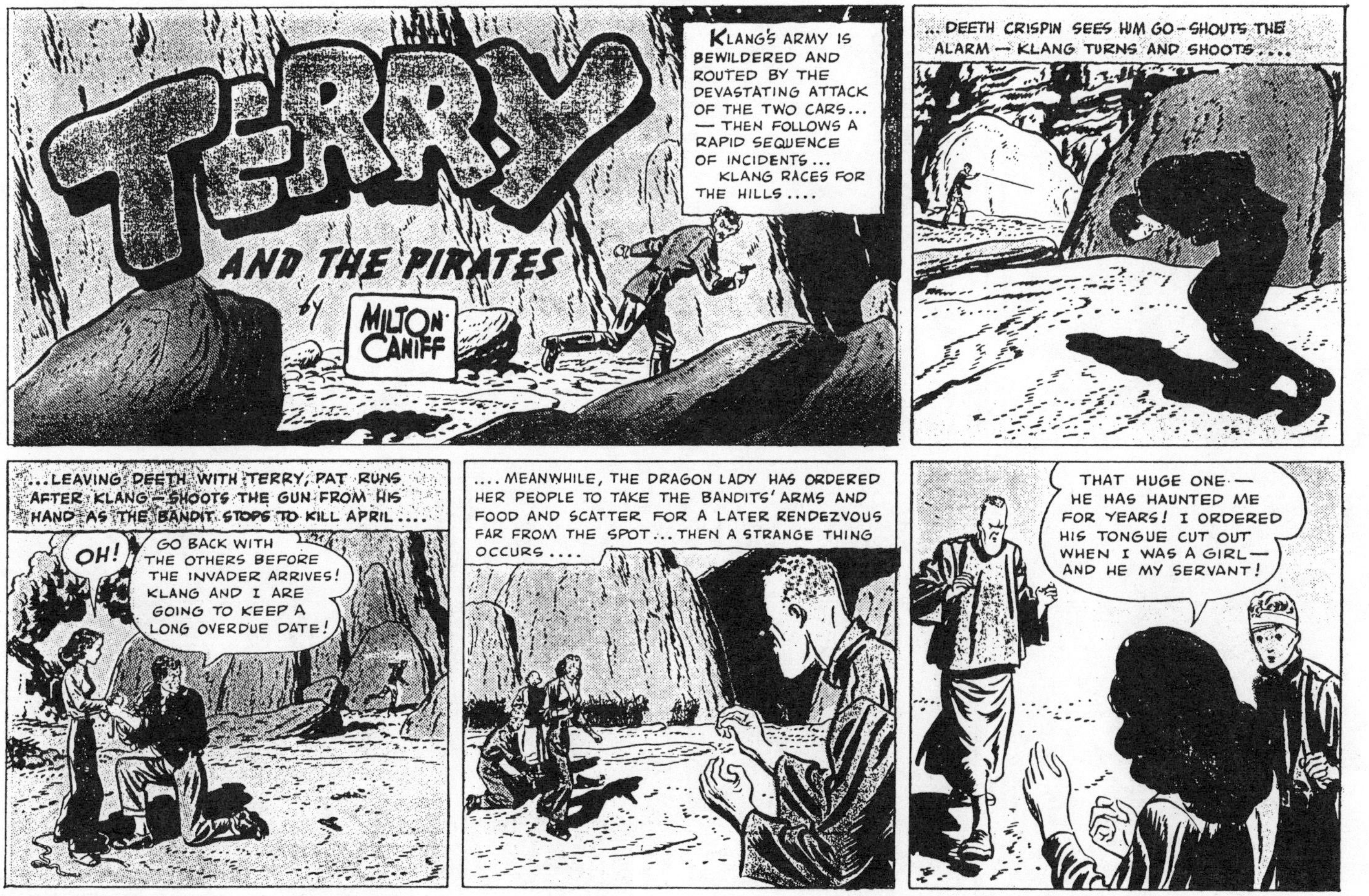
TERRY AND THE PIRATES
by MILTON CANIFF
KLANG'S ARMY IS BEWILDERED AND ROUTED BY THE DEVASTATING ATTACK OF THE TWO CARS... — THEN FOLLOWS A RAPID SEQUENCE OF INCIDENTS... KLANG RACES FOR THE HILLS....
... DEETH CRISPIN SEES HIM GO-SHOUTS THE ALARM — KLANG TURNS AND SHOOTS....
...LEAVING DEETH WITH TERRY, PAT RUNS AFTER KLANG—SHOOTS THE GUN FROM HIS HAND AS THE BANDIT STOPS TO KILL APRIL....
OH!
GO BACK WITH THE OTHERS BEFORE THE INVADER ARRIVES! KLANG AND I ARE GOING TO KEEP A LONG OVERDUE DATE!
.... MEANWHILE, THE DRAGON LADY HAS ORDERED HER PEOPLE TO TAKE THE BANDITS' ARMS AND FOOD AND SCATTER FOR A LATER RENDEZVOUS FAR FROM THE SPOT... THEN A STRANGE THING OCCURS....
THAT HUGE ONE — HE HAS HAUNTED ME FOR YEARS! I ORDERED HIS TONGUE CUT OUT WHEN I WAS A GIRL— AND HE MY SERVANT!

HOKIE SMOKY! CONNIE NOT REALIZE DLAGON LADY NOT SEE BIG STOOPER IN ALL TIME WE KNOW HIM!
—AND HE DIDN'T KNOW WHO WE MEANT WHEN WE TALKED OF THE DRAGON LADY — SHE GOT THE NAME LATER IN LIFE!
HE WILL CRUSH ME WITH THOSE HANDS! STOP HIM — OR I'LL SHOOT!
NO CAN SHOOT BIG STOOPER!
IF HE TOUCHES ME, HE WILL BREAK ME IN TWO! HE IS THE ONE PERSON IN THE WORLD I FEAR! STOP HIM!
THE ROPE THAT DID THE DAMAGE TO KLANG'S ARMY HAS BEEN USED TO TIE UP THE DAZED BANDITS — THE DRAGON LADY LEAPS BEHIND THE WHEEL OF ONE OF THE IDLING CARS — JAMS IT INTO GEAR AND ROARS AWAY....
ALARM! MOVING CLOUD OF DUST ON ROAD FLOM INVADER CAMP!
UNABLE TO SEE THE APPROACHING ENEMY FROM GROUND LEVEL, THE DRAGON LADY HURTLES DIRECTLY INTO THEIR PATH... WITH THE THROTTLE WIDE-OPEN....
10-22
IT ALL HAPPENED SO SUDDENLY — THE DRAGON LADY YELLED THAT IT WAS SHE WHO ORDERED BIG STOOP'S TONGUE CUT OUT YEARS AGO!
THEN HER JUMP IN GASSY-WAGON AN' GO SCOOTIN' JUS' BEFORE STOOPER GOT BIG MITTS ON SHE NECK!
10-23
Reg. U. S. Pat. Off.: Copyright, 1939, by News Syndicate Co., Inc.
STUFF'S COMIN' TOO FAST! YOU RESCUE US — THEN — BAM — THE DRAGON LADY IS BEATING IT BECAUSE SHE'S REALLY SCARED OF STOOP!
MISSY APLIL AN' MIST' PAT BEST COME SOON OR WE ALL IN WORSE PICKLEMENT THAN NOW-TIME!
—YEAH — ONE OF THE DRAGON LADY'S MEN SAID THERE WAS DUST RISING ON THE ROAD FROM THE INVADER'S CAMP!
GIVE LISTEN! —CONNIE HEAR BIG SHOOTIN'S UP VALLEY!
INVADERS COME SUDDEN IN WAR WAGONS! — CATCHUM MASTER DLAGON LADY! WHITE MANS RUN BEFORE SAME HAPPEN TO SELF!!
MILTON CANIFF
IF INVADER GENTS HAVE CATCHUM DLAGON LADY THEY SOON-TIME ON HEELS OF US! NO CAN HELP SHE NOW!... BETTER SKEEDOODLE!
—BUT APRIL AN' PAT ARE MISSIN'! —CAN'T GO WITHOUT THEM!
10-24
MISSY APLIL WITH MIST' PAT! WE MUS' CARRY MIST' DEET' CLISPIN NUMBER TREE TO SAFELY PLACE!
I KNOW, BUT NOT WITHOUT APRIL AN' PAT!
Reg. U. S. Pat. Off.: Copyright, 1939, by News Syndicate Co., Inc.
BUT THEY KNOW RIVER CLOSE BY! US GOTTA GO — OR GET COTCHED!
NO?
MILTON CANIFF

DOESN'T MATTER HOW FAR YOU RUN, MISTER K. I'VE GOT LOTS OF TIME!
10-25
Reg. U. S. Pat. Off.; Copyright, 1939, by News Syndicate Co., Inc.
APRIL WILL GET AWAY WITH THE OTHERS IN THAT INVADER CAR — SO YOU AND I CAN SETTLE OUR LITTLE SCORE UP HERE ALL ALONE!
SHOOTING BELOW! THAT MEANS THE INVADER HAS ARRIVED! MY FRIENDS WILL GET AWAY — BUT YOU WON'T, MY PANIC-STRICKEN FRIEND!
... FINALLY HIT A BLANK WALL, DIDN'T YOU? JUST WAIT THERE, SONNY BOY! YOUR LESSON IN GOOD MANNERS WILL START ANY MINUTE NOW!
MILTON CANIFF

OH, LOOK! HE'S FOUND A SHILLALAH!
10-26
Reg. U. S. Pat. Off.; Copyright, 1939, by News Syndicate Co., Inc.
LET'S SORTA TOSS OUT THE PICK HANDLE AN' KEEP IT PERSONAL! IT'S SO MUCH COZIER! STAND UP!!
MILTON CANIFF

NOW HE'S USING IRISH CONFETTI!
10-27
I TELL YOU, YOU'VE GOT TO BE BORN TO THESE THINGS!
OOMP!
Reg. U. S. Pat. Off.; Copyright, 1939, by News Syndicate Co., Inc.
AND THAT'S HOW IT FEELS TO GET KICKED WHEN YOUR HANDS ARE TIED!
MILTON CANIFF

THAT'S FOR TERRY AND APRIL ...
10-28
Reg. U. S. Pat. Off.; Copyright, 1939, by News Syndicate Co., Inc.
THAT'S FOR DEETH CRISPIN!..
THAT'S FOR ME!!...
MILTON CANIFF
... AND THAT'S FOR JUST BEING ALIVE IN THE FIRST PLACE!

TERRY AND THE PIRATES
by MILTON CANIFF
GOLLY — WE JUST GOT OUT OF THERE IN TIME! THE DRAGON LADY MUST HAVE SLAMMED RIGHT INTO THOSE INVADER CARS!
IS SO! US BEST HIDE IN DAY-TIMES AN' SCOOT IN NIGHT OR US GET KETCHED ALSO! THEM SKIN US LIVELY IF EVER GET HANDS ON!
GEE, MY HEAD HURTS —AN' WHEN I THINK WHAT HAPPENED TO DEETH... AN' I WONDER WHERE APRIL AND PAT ARE — AN' BIG STOOP TURNS OUT TO BE THE ONLY PERSON THE DRAGON LADY FEARS... I'M ALL JUMBLED UP!
NO STEW IN OWN JUICY, MIST' TERRY! US GET MIST' DEET' TO RIVER, CHOP CHOP! MIST' PAT GO FETCH MISSY APLIL! HIM SEE HER TO SAFELY, YOU BET-ME!
MEANWHILE — ON A ROCK FAR FROM THE BATTLE GROUND....
I SENT APRIL BACK— SO SHE'S SAFE WITH TERRY— NOW WE CAN PLAY A LITTLE TWO-HANDED POKER ALL BY OURSELVES!
DON'T HIT ME AGAIN...
I HAVE MONEY! IT'S ALL YOURS IF YOU SET ME FREE!
IT'S MINE, ANYWAY, YOU DOPE! —YOU TOOK IT FROM ME WHEN I STUMBLED INTO YOUR AMBUSH!
10-29
OH, GREAT DAY IN TH' MORNIN'! I CAN'T WATCH THIS AN' STILL BE A LADY!!

10-30
IF YOU DON'T KNOW WHEN YOU'RE LICKED, I'LL SHOW YOU – THE ONLY WAY YOU'D UNDERSTAND!
NOW GET ON YOUR HANDS AND KNEES! I'M GOING TO KICK YOU ALL THE WAY TO THE CHINESE ARMY! THEY CAN EXTERMINATE THEIR OWN RATS!
OH, I WAS AFRAID YOU'D KILL HIM RIGHT BEFORE MY EYES!
WH...
MILTON CANIFF
Reg. U. S. Pat. Off.: Copyright, 1939, by News Syndicate Co., Inc.

10-31
Reg. U. S. Pat. Off.: Copyright, 1939, by News Syndicate Co., Inc.
MILTON CANIFF

11-1
OH, MERCY GUIDE ME! I DID AN AWFUL THING!
STOP WAILIN' AND GRAB THAT MONEY BELT KLANG DROPPED!
BUT WHAT GOOD...?
SO I CAN HAUL MYSELF UP! BRACE YOURSELF AGAINST A ROCK AND HOLD ONE END!
I DON'T THINK THIS WILL WORK!
BUT IT'S ALL WE HAVE! HURRY!
Reg. U. S. Pat. Off.: Copyright, 1939, by News Syndicate Co., Inc.
THEN YOU DON'T WANT ME T' USE TH' ROPE I BROUGHT FROM WHERE KLANG HAD ME TIED?
OOOOOHHH
MILTON CANIFF

11-2
Reg. U. S. Pat. Off.: Copyright, 1939, by News Syndicate Co., Inc.
MR. RYAN – ARE YOU DEAD, OR SOMETHIN'?
NO – MUCH TO MY SURPRISE!
OH, GLORY SAVE ME! HE'S GONNA DO ME HARM!
DON'T BE SO SECOND ACT CLIMAX – I WANT YOU TO RUB MY ARMS! – THEY'RE NUMB!
OH!
MILTON CANIFF

THAT'S BETTER! THANKS! IN FACT, THANKS FOR... WELL, EVERYTHING YOU DID!
IT WAS SINFUL—BUT YOU WERE IN DANGER—AN' THAT KLANG WAS SO EVIL! ...MY BUT YOU'RE STRONG!
11-3
NEVER FORGET THE RIGHT THINGS TO SAY TO THE GENTLEMAN, DO YOU, JASMINE?
IF YOU'RE GONNA CARRY ON ABOUT MY WAY O'TALKIN' I RECKON I'LL HAVE T' JUS' HATE YOU SOME!
Reg. U.S. Pat. Off.: Copyright, 1939, by News Syndicate Co., Inc.
SAVE IT, KITTEN! WE'RE TOO FAR FROM CIVILIZATION FOR PERSONAL FEELINGS! WHY DID YOU FOLLOW US INSTEAD OF GOING WITH TERRY, AS I TOLD YOU?
I JUS' KNEW Y'ALL WERE GONNA FIGHT—AN' COURSE I KNEW YOU'D WIN...
—I RECKONED YOU'D BE MAROONED UP HERE ALL TUCKERED OUT—SO I PUT SOME O' KLANG'S FOOD AN' WATER IN A POKE—PICKED UP THAT ROPE—AN' JUS' TAGGED ALONG!
SUGAH PLUM, I'M BEGINNING TO UNDERSTAND HOW THE CONFEDERATE ARMY HELD OUT SO LONG! WILL YOU DO ME THE HONOR OF TAKING MY ARM AS WE WALK OVER TO THOSE VICTUALS?
MILTON CANIFF

NO HARM MAY BEFALL US—WE HAVE DINED WELL!
THAT'S RIGHT CLEVER! I'LL JUS' TUCK THIS EXTRA FOOD AWAY FOR WHEN WE GET HUNGRY AGAIN!
11-4
Reg. U.S. Pat. Off.: Copyright, 1939, by News Syndicate Co., Inc.
...AND WE'LL TAKE THE MONEY BELT KLANG SWIPED FROM ME AT THE AMBUSH! YOU ALL SET TO HIKE?
I RECKON SO!
YOU LOOK AWFULLY DARN GAY FOR THE PICKLE WE'RE IN! DO YOU REALIZE WE'RE LOST IN THE MIDDLE OF A WAR TORN COUNTRY WITH MIGHTY SLIM CHANCES OF GETTING OUT ALIVE?
WHY, CERTAINLY! —BUT I'M SURE THE OTHERS ARE SAFE... AN' MOS' GIRLS WOULD BE BUSTIN' WITH PLEASURE AT HAVIN' A STRONG, HANDSOME GENTLEMAN TO SEE THEM THROUGH UNTOLD DANGERS
HMMM!
MILTON CANIFF

TERRY AND THE PIRATES by MILTON CANIFF
Reg. U.S. Pat. Off. Copyright, 1939, by News Syndicate Co., Inc.
MR. RYAN, I HOPE YOU DON'T RESENT MY POKIN' ALONG AFTER YOU AN' THAT AWFUL KLANG MAN, INSTEAD OF JOINING THE OTHERS, AS YOU TOLD ME!
I COULD HARDLY RESENT IT... WHEN YOU KEPT KLANG FROM PITCHING ME OFF THAT CLIFF... AND WHEN YOU HAD THE FORESIGHT TO BRING ALONG FOOD AND WATER—BECAUSE YOU KNEW WE'D BE LOST IN THIS FORSAKEN COUNTRY...
THEN WHY ARE YOU SO GLUMPY? I DECLARE, YOU LOOK AS IF YOU HAVE FIDGETS IN TH' HEAD!
THIS IS BAD TERRITORY, KITTEN! WHOEVER WE STUMBLE INTO WE'RE IN HOT WATER! WE'VE GOT TO SLIP BACK THROUGH THE WAR ZONE—AND IT'S GOING TO BE TOUGH SLIPPING!
WELL, I JUS' CAN'T GET IN A PET OVER THAT—WHEN I HAVE YOU TO PROTECT ME!
YOU'VE BEEN READING TOO MANY BOOKS, SUGAH! IN REAL LIFE IT DOESN'T ALWAYS END SO HAPPILY! HEY! THERE'S A BREAK!
WH-WHAT?
A STREAM! WATER! WE CAN SCRUB OFF THE GRIME—I FEEL I'VE JUST STEPPED OUT OF A NICE MELLOW OLD HOG PEN!
OH, GLORY BE! ... I MEAN... OH, MERCY ME... I—I...

NOW DON'T BE COY, MISS KANE! YOU'LL HAVE PLENTY OF PRIVACY! YOU USE THIS POOL BY THE ROCK! I'LL BE DOWNSTREAM—BUT WITHIN SHOUTING DISTANCE! YELL WHEN YOU'RE READY!
WH-WHY, YES—OF COURSE!
NOTHING LIKE NICE CLEAN SAND TO TAKE THE HIDE OFF... BUT YOU CAN'T HAVE EVERYTHING!
MUCH LATER
WHERE THE DEVIL'S APRIL? DO WOMEN TAKE THIS MUCH TIME TO DRESS EVEN IN SUCH A WILDERNESS? WHAT'S THAT?
BLOG! GLOB!
YEEOW!
BLOO.. CAN'T SEE... BLUG...
NO—BUT I CAN SEE —VERY CLEARLY
11-5
LISTEN, KITTEN, YOU DON'T NEED MUD PACKS TO IMPROVE YOUR COMPLEXION... ESPECIALLY MADE OF THIS CHINESE CLAY THAT HARDENS LIKE CEMENT! UNCLE PAT WILL CONCEDE THAT YOU'RE BEAUTIFUL—BEFORE YOU TRY IT AGAIN AND I HAVE TO BLAST!

IT WAS RIGHT GALLANT TH' WAY YOU STOOD GUARD DOWNSTREAM WHILE I HAD MY BATH, MR. RYAN!
I SPENT THE TIME IRONING OUT THE KINKS FROM THAT FIGHT WITH KLANG! ... WHY DO YOU CALL ME MISTER?
11-6
Reg. U. S. Pat. Off.; Copyright, 1939, by News Syndicate Co., Inc.
I RECKON IT'S 'CAUSE YOU'RE SO MUCH MORE MATURE THAN SILLY OL' ME! —YOU'RE SUCH A MAN OF THE WORLD, SORTA!
YOU MEAN BECAUSE I'VE BEEN AROUND A BIT?
YES... AN' YOU'VE LEARNED SO MUCH ABOUT PEOPLE— 'SPECIALLY WOMEN!
HMMM...
LISTEN, KITTEN KANE, IF I HAD LEARNED AS MUCH ABOUT WOMEN IN THE YEARS I'VE BEEN ALIVE AS YOU KNEW ABOUT MEN THE DAY YOU WERE BORN—I'D CONSIDER MYSELF A SMART INDIAN!
MILTON CANIFF

GREAT DAY, WE'VE WALKED A MILLION MILES! DO YOU RECKON WE'LL EVER REACH A TOWN?
IF YOU HAD BEEN A GOOD GIRL SCOUT INSTEAD OF BREAKING YOUNG MEN'S HEARTS, YOU'D KNOW THAT RIVERS ALWAYS LEAD TO CIVILIZATION!
11-7
Reg. U. S. Pat. Off.; Copyright, 1939, by News Syndicate Co., Inc.
WHY, THAT'S DOWNRIGHT RUDE OF YOU! I NEVER DID BREAK BOYS' HEARTS! YOU KNOW RIGHT WELL THAT A PLAIN LITTLE THING LIKE ME COULD NEVER GET ANY BEAUX!
THEN WHAT ARE ALL THOSE SCALPS HANGING FROM YOUR BELT?
WHERE?...OH, DAWGONE YOU, PATRICK RYAN! YOU DEVILED ME INTO LOOKIN' AT MY BELT! I RECKON YOU THINK THAT'S CLEVER!
NOW, DON'T YOU FRET, KITTEN! I KNOW THE RIGHT ANSWER TO YOUR SAYING YOU'RE TOO PLAIN! I JUST WANTED TO GIVE YOU A CHANGE OF PACE ON THE STANDARD REPLY! FACT IS, YOUR MODESTY IS MOS' BECOMIN'—AN' IT'S COMMON' TALK THAT YOU'RE TH' PRETTIEST GAL NORTH OF JONESBORO!
I'M SO MAD I COULD SNIP YOU!
MILTON CANIFF

COME ON, WOMAN, GET OVER YOUR GLOOMPS AND WHIP UP SOME VITTLES, OR I'LL TRADE YOU IN ON A CAMEL!
YOU'RE THE RUDEST MAN I EVER DID KNOW! BACK HOME, IF ANYONE TREATED ME SO MEAN, MY DADDY WOULD...
11-8
Reg. U. S. Pat. Off.: Copyright, 1939, by News Syndicate Co., Inc.
...YOUR DADDY WOULD THANK ME FOR BRINGING YOU BACK! —WHICH I INTEND TO DO! RIGHT NOW, GETTING YOU FED IS PART OF THE PROCEDURE! COME ON!
I WON'T DO IT! YOU MADE FUN OF ME... YOU—YOU—YANKEE!
I'M PROPERLY CRUSHED, BUT UNTIL WE GET TO WHERE YOU CAN FLOUNCE OUT AFTER YOUR BIG SPEECH, YOU'RE GOING TO EAT WITH ME!
OH!
OH, MR. RYAN—YOU'RE SO STRONG!
MILTON CANIFF

MR. RYAN, I'VE BEEN THINKIN' IT OVER....I WAS SORTA SHARP WITH YOU... IF YOU'D CARE TO FORGET OUR SPAT, I'D NOT BE ANGRY ANYMORE!
SURE, KITTEN! IT'S PRETTY DULL SITTING HERE LOOKING INTO THE FIRE WITH NO ONE TO TALK TO! I APOLOGIZE FOR BEING RUDE, TOO!
11-9
Reg. U. S. Pat. Off.: Copyright, 1939, by News Syndicate Co., Inc.
I'M SURE YOU DIDN'T MEAN TO BE STINGIN' IN YOUR REMARKS! YOU'RE SO KIND AN' UNDERSTANDIN'! BRRRR...IT'S MIGHTY CHILLY!
BETTER CURL UP AGAINST THE WARM ROCK AND GO TO SLEEP! TOUGH DAY TOMORROW!
AREN'T YOU GOIN' TO SLEEP?
GOT TO KEEP THE FIRE ALIVE OR WE'D BOTH FREEZE UP SOLID!
I'M SO SHIVERY... D-DO YOU RECKON IT WOULD BE CONSIDERED IMPROPER IF I KINDA SAT—WELL, SORTA CLOSE TO YOU?
WELL—THE BATS MIGHT THINK IT ODD—BUT I BELIEVE WE CAN RISK IT—THIS ONCE!
MILTON CANIFF

THIS IS NICE.... DO YOU SUPPOSE TERRY AND DEETH AND THE DRAGON LADY ARE ALL RIGHT—WHEREVER THEY ARE?
POOR KID—SHE DOESN'T KNOW ABOUT DEETH! NO USE TO SPRING IT NOW...
SURE! THEY KNOW HOW TO TAKE CARE OF THEMSELVES!
11-10
...WHAT CONCERNS ME IS THE TORTURE YOUR BROTHER AND PARENTS ARE GOING THROUGH—WORRYING ABOUT YOU!
OH, THEY'LL FRET—BUT MUMS IS SORTA PSYCHIC! SHE'LL KNOW I'M SAFE! THAT'S A MERCY!
Reg. U. S. Pat. Off.: Copyright, 1939, by News Syndicate Co., Inc.
BUT YOU'RE NOT SAFE, KITTEN! WE'RE IN THE MIDDLE OF A WAR—BESIDES, HEAVEN KNOWS WHAT OTHER DANGERS ROAM OUT THERE IN THE NIGHT!
MILTON CANIFF
WHY, NONE OF THAT FIDGETS ME A MITE! I KNOW THERE ISN'T ANYTHING IN TH' WORLD SO THREATENIN' THAT YOU COULDN'T SMITE IT DOWN!
...WHAT ARE YOU THINKIN'?
...JUST WONDERING HOW THE SOUTH COULD POSSIBLY HAVE LOST THE WAR BETWEEN THE STATES!

WAKE UP, SUGAH! TIME FOR YOUR MORNING WALK!
OH, MISERY! I'M RUSTY ALL OVER! MY OL' JOINTS ARE MOANIN' AT ME!
11-11
A LITTLE EXERCISE WILL LOOSEN YOU UP!
I DECLARE, I JUS' CAN'T STEP AN INCH—D-DO YOU RECKON IT'D FRET YOU T' CARRY ME A WAY?
OH, NO! YOU PICK 'EM UP AN' LAY EM DOWN! THAT SUN WILL SOON UNRAVEL THE KINKS! HIKE!
I SWEAR I'LL NEVER GET MARRIED—IF ALL MEN ARE AS UNREASONABLE AS YOU IN TH' MORNIN'! I RECKON THERE'S JUS' NO CHIVALRY ANYMORE!
SHUSH, KITTEN! WE'VE GOT TO STEP TO GET SAFELY THROUGH TO CIVILIZATION!
MILTON CANIFF
Reg. U. S. Pat. Off.: Copyright, 1939, by News Syndicate Co., Inc.

TERRY AND THE PIRATES
by MILTON CANIFF
Reg. U. S. Pat. Off.; Copyright, 1939, by News Syndicate Co., Inc.
I'M NOT FIBBIN', MR. RYAN! MY OL' FEET ARE JUS' A PAIR OF FLAMIN' TORCHES HANGIN' FROM MY ANKLES!
I KNOW, KITTEN! WE'LL STOP AND GIVE 'EM A SWIM!
OH, WHAT A MERCY! YOU SAY ALL RIVERS LEAD TO CIVILIZATION — BUT I'M RIGHT CONTENT THAT THIS ONE'S JUS' WET AN' COOL! OOOOOOHH!
HAVE YOUR FUN, SUGAH... WE'VE GOT TO MAKE TIME OUT OF THIS WAR ZONE — OR WE'LL BE PUSHIN' UP CHINESE TIGER LILIES!
PLEASE COME AN' SIT A SPELL, MR. RYAN! 'COURSE YOU KNOW BEST 'BOUT MOVIN' ON AN' ALL — BUT YOU WERE UP ALL LAST NIGHT TENDIN' TH' FIRE SO I COULD SLEEP... JUS' REST A MITE!
I AM DROOPY! DON'T LET ME FALL ASLEEP, THOUGH.... WE'VE GOT TO MOVE ON...
POOR BABY... HE'S PLAIN EXHAUSTED... NO HARM LETTING HIM DOZE A BIT!... MY, HE'S A HAN'SOME MAN... WONDER IF HE'D PAY ME SOME MIND IF I WERE OLDER... SUN'S SO WARM... KINDA DROWSY.....
HUH — WH' TIME IS IT? HEY!
OH!
OH, MR. RYAN, I DIDN'T MEAN TO DOZE... HONEST, I...
EASY, KITTEN! THESE GENTS DON'T SEEM BELLIGERENT! — SOME SORT OF MONKS....
YOU WIFE?
OH, MR. RYAN, HE ASKED IF I AM YOUR WIFE! ISN'T THAT COMICAL?
YEAH — I'M BUSTIN' LAUGHING! ...YOU B'LONG FOOD? — YOU KNOW... EAT! WE PAY!
BLING 'LONG WIFE! GET EAT!
WE GATHER BAGGAGE! YOU GO — WE FOLLOW, CHOP, CHOP!
HOW NICE THAT THOSE MEN UNDERSTAND! BUT THEY THINK I'M YOUR WIFE — WHAT FUN!
LISTEN CLOSELY, APRIL! WHEN I GIVE YOU AN ORDER, OBEY IT INSTANTLY! AND KEEP YOUR EYE ON ME FOR SIGNALS — DON'T FORGET!!
ARE YOU TRYIN' TO BE DOMINATIN' JUS' BECAUSE THAT NICE MAN THINKS WE'RE MARRIED?
11-12
NO, MY LITTLE PLUM-PIE... IT'S BECAUSE OUR NICE MONK FRIENDS ARE CARRYING RIFLES UNDER THEIR ROBES!

...THOSE MEN IN THE ROBES COMIN' ON US SO SUDDEN LIKE!... MY OL' HEART'S STILL IN MY WINDPIPE!
THEY'VE OFFERED TO TAKE US TO SOME FOOD—AND THEY SEEM PEACEFUL—BUT THERE ARE RIFLES UNDER THOSE ROBES!
11-13
THEY MUST NOT BE PEEVED AT US—OR THEY'D HAVE SHOT US BEFORE THIS!... I'M STILL LAUGHIN' AT THEM CALLIN' ME YOUR WIFE!
IT'S NOT STRANGE! WOMEN MARRY QUITE EARLY IN LIFE OUT HERE!
Reg. U. S. Pat. Off. Copyright, 1939, by News Syndicate Co., Inc.
YOU'VE BEEN QUIET FOR A MILE! ...WORRIED?
MERCY, NO! I WAS JUS' THINKIN'... THE CHINESE HAVE SOME VERY INTERESTIN' CUSTOMS!
MILTON CANIFF

GREAT DAY, MR. RYAN, THOSE MEN IN TH' ROBES ARE TAKIN' US TO CIVILIZATION, SURE NUFF!
LOOKS LIKE A BIG FARM! ....THAT BARBED WIRE IS OMINOUS!
BLING 'LONG WIFE!
11-14
HE STILL THINKS I'M YOUR WIFE! I DECLARE—IT DOESN'T MATTER WHAT HE THINKS—AS LONG AS WE GET FED!—OH, IT'S RAININ'!
I WAS AFRAID OF THAT!
I SWEAR YOU'RE ALWAYS STEWIN' 'BOUT SOMETHIN'! WHAT'S SO FRETTIN' 'BOUT A LITTLE RAIN?
IT WON'T BE A LITTLE RAIN, KITTEN... IF IT'S A HEAVY MONSOON, WE'LL BE STUCK HERE FOR A GOOD LONG STRETCH...
MERCY! I'D BE MIGHTY FRIGHTENED ...IF I WERE ALONE!
MILTON CANIFF
Reg. U. S. Pat. Off.: Copyright, 1939, by News Syndicate Co., Inc.

WHAT ARE THEY PALAVERIN' WITH THOSE MEN AT THE GATE FOR? WE'LL CATCH OUR DEATH O' SOAKIN'!
IN THESE WILD AND WOOLLY PARTS, YOU DON'T JUST TAKE IN EVERY STRANGER WHO POPS ALONG!
11-15
YOU COME! BLING WIFE!
GUESS I'M INVITED, TOO! RUN, MR. RYAN!
OOPS!
Reg. U. S. Pat. Off.: Copyright, 1939, by News Syndicate Co., Inc.
MERCY, HONEY! DID YOU HURT YOURSELF?
NO—BUT I'LL ACT HURT! ...JUST WANTED AN EXCUSE TO BUMP THAT CART! THERE'S A MACHINE GUN UNDER THE INNOCENT LOOKING COVER! I DON'T KNOW WHAT WE'RE IN FOR, KITTEN, SO KEEP YOUR WITS SHARP AND YOUR CHIN UP!
OH!
COME! —IS WET!
MILTON CANIFF

YOU HURT ?
ANKLE TURNED! IS NOTHING!
YOU AN' WIFE WAIT!
11-16
WE GOT HERE JUST IN TIME, APRIL! IT'S POURING OUTSIDE! NOT A BAD PLACE, HUH?
YOU NEEDN'T TRY T'BE SO CHEERFUL, MR. RYAN! I KNOW YOU'RE WORRIED 'BOUT OL' ME!
Reg. U. S. Pat. Off.: Copyright, 1939, by News Syndicate Co., Inc.
WELL, FRANKLY, I --- HEY! YOU NOTICE ANYTHING?
MMM! —I SURELY DO!—AN' IT'S COMIN' THIS WAY!
MILTON CANIFF
MR. RYAN, MUCH AS I REGRET T' TAKE ISSUE WITH YOU—ANYONE WHO CAN DISH UP VICTUALS LIKE THAT COULD MEAN NO HARM TO ANYONE!

WHY– HE'S ONLY SETTIN' ONE PLACE!
HE THINKS YOU'RE MY WIFE–AND CHINESE WIVES DON'T EAT WITH THEIR MEN! HEY! WE BOTH EAT HERE! AMERICAN WAY! YOU CATCH?
11-17
MERCY SAVE US! I THOUGHT FOR A MINUTE ONE OF US WAS DUE FOR FASTIN'! ... PARDON ME TILL DESSERT!
LATER
GREAT DAY IN TH' MORNIN'! I'M FIT T' BUST! I'VE EATEN DISGRACEFUL MUCH... SO MUCH I'M... GETTIN... SLEEPY!...
FUNNY... SO AM I... HOLY SMOKE... I'M STUPID... WE'VE ... WE'VE BEEN DRUGGED.... TRY... TO... GET ... SOME ... AIR...
Reg. U. S. Pat. Off. Copyright, 1939, by News Syndicate Co., Inc.
MILTON CANIFF
AH, THEY CEASE TO STRUGGLE! LET US PROCEED!

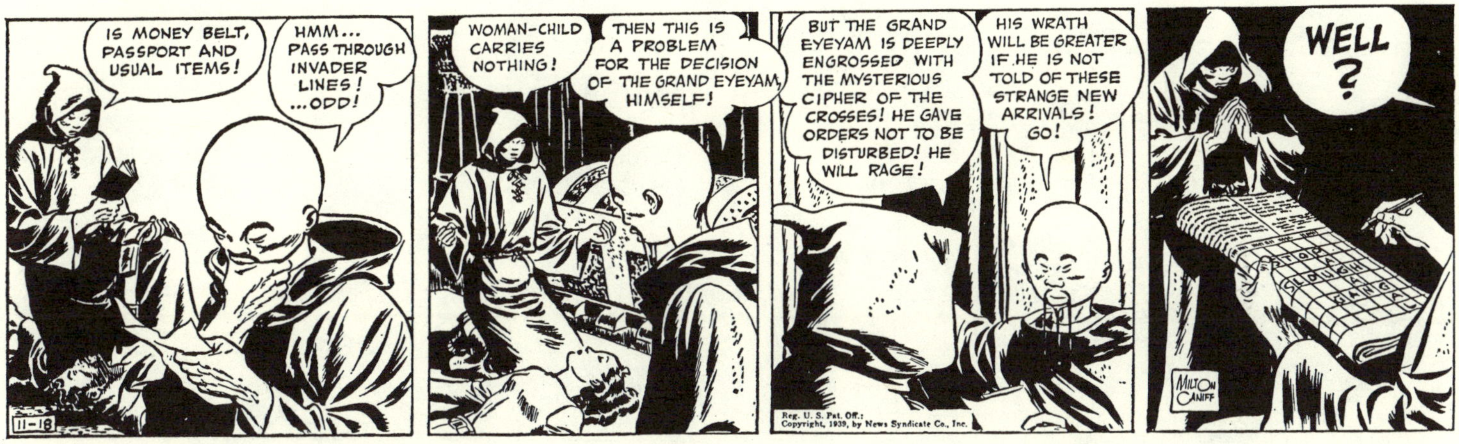

IS MONEY BELT, PASSPORT AND USUAL ITEMS!
HMM... PASS THROUGH INVADER LINES! ...ODD!
11-18
WOMAN-CHILD CARRIES NOTHING!
THEN THIS IS A PROBLEM FOR THE DECISION OF THE GRAND EYEYAM HIMSELF!
BUT THE GRAND EYEYAM IS DEEPLY ENGROSSED WITH THE MYSTERIOUS CIPHER OF THE CROSSES! HE GAVE ORDERS NOT TO BE DISTURBED! HE WILL RAGE!
HIS WRATH WILL BE GREATER IF HE IS NOT TOLD OF THESE STRANGE NEW ARRIVALS! GO!
Reg. U. S. Pat. Off.; Copyright, 1939, by News Syndicate Co., Inc.
WELL ?
MILTON CANIFF

TERRY AND THE PIRATES
by MILTON CANIFF
ALLOW THESE ODD NEWCOMERS TO SLEEP UNTIL THE DRUG WEARS OFF! I HAVE SENT FOR THE GRAND EYEYAM TO MAKE A DECISION!
OOOOH...
... IS IT MORNING –OR IS THIS THE END OF THE LINE?
WHAT IN TH' WORLD HAPPENED?
THE LAST THING I CAN REMEMBER, OUR GUN-TOTING, ROBED FRIENDS BROUGHT US TO THIS PLACE–WE ATE A WHALE OF A MEAL –THEN SOMEONE STOLE MY MIND!
I RECKON YOU WERE RIGHT 'BOUT THIS PLACE BEIN' DANGER--- OH!
AH, IT IS PLAIN THAT THE HONORED GUESTS AWAKEN FROM THEIR EXHAUSTED SLUMBER!
EXHAUSTED SLUMBER, MY GREAT AUNT! WE WERE VERY NEATLY 'DRUGGED! NOW, IF YOU WILL TELL US WHAT WE OWE YOU.... OH, I SEE YOU LIFTED MY MONEY BELT, TOO! WELL, IT'S YOUR ROUND, UP TO NOW!
THE ESTEEMED VISITOR'S VOICE CONTAINS A NOTE OF ANGER! CAN IT BE THAT OUR POOR HOSPITALITY IS INADEQUATE?

THE GRUB WAS OKAY —BUT WE CAN'T WORK UP A FANCY FOR BEING DRUGGED AND ROLLED FOR OUR DOUGH!
THIS IGNORANT ONE'S KNOWLEDGE OF ENGLISH IS TOO MEAGRE TO UNDERSTAND WHAT YOU SAY!
LISTEN, MISTER CUE-BALL, YOU KNOW WHAT I MEAN! I WON'T TRY TO BATTLE A WAY OUT OF THIS ARSENAL... KEEP THE MONEY- BUT GIVE ME MY PAPERS AND WE'LL GO!
THIS HUMBLE PERSON IS BUT A SECONDARY FIGURE! THE GRAND EYEYAM WILL SPEAK WITH YOU!
THE GRAND EYEYAM? THAT'S A NEW ONE! JUST WHO IS THIS EXALTED NIBS —WHO DEALS OUT MICKEY FINNS TO PASSING TOURISTS?
SUCH BLASPHEMY MAY COST YOU DEARLY, MY HASTY ONE!
LOWER ALL PROFANE EYES! THE EXALTED ONE IS ABOUT TO ENTER!
NUTS!
OH, MY!
I WARNED YOU —YOU WILL BE PUNISHED...
TAKE YOUR HANDS OFF ME, MISTER CUE-BALL—OR I'LL SINK YOU IN THE SIDE POCKET!
MISTER CUE-BALL?
11-19
BLOW ME TOPPER! HI'VE BEEN TRYIN' FOR MONTHS T' THINK OF A NAME FER THAT DROOP! —MIGHTA KNOWN HIT'D TYKE TH' SECOND BEST CHECKER PLAYER IN CHINA TO 'IT ON IT! WELCOME T' ME DIGGIN'S, PATRICK RYAN!
CAP'N BLAZE!!
OH, EXALTED ONE... THIS MAN AND HIS WIFE...
DON'T YE SPUTTER AROUND ABOUT THIS BLOKE! HI'VE KNOWN TH' 'ANDSOME SINNER SINCE BEFORE HI 'AD THE BLINKIN' EVIL LUCK T' VIEW YER PASTY FACE FER THE FIRST TIME!
11-20
Reg. U. S. Pat. Off.; Copyright, 1939, by News Syndicate Co., Inc.
CAPTAIN BLAZE! ... AM I DREAMING?
BLIGH'ME, NO, PATRICK RYAN! HI'M RIGHT BEFORE YE IN TH' FLESH—AN' BLAWSTED PLENTY OF IT, HI MUST SAY! HAWHAWHAWHAW!
BUT WE JUST WOKE UP... THE FOOD WE ATE MUST HAVE BEEN DRUGGED...
HO! THEY GAVE YE TH' BEAUTY SLEEP, EH! YE'LL 'AVE T' FORGIVE 'EM, IT'S ROUTINE WELCOME 'ERE! THAT'S 'OW WE LEARNS OUR VISITORS' BUSINESS!
...BUT THIS 'ERE AIN'T NO PLACE FER HONORED GUESTS LIKE YOU! BRING YER OL' LADY AN' COME INTO ME SANCTUM SANCTORIOUS!
?
MILTON CANIFF
WOT'S EATIN' YER OL' LADY?
YOU SEE, SHE'S NOT MY WIFE... YOUR MEN JUST TOOK IT FOR GRANTED THAT WE WERE MARRIED!
11-21
WELL, BLOW ME TOPPER, MISS, HI THOUGHT YE'D LED THIS 'ERE 'ANDSOME 'ARRY TO THE ALTAR! HI TAKE HIT, THEN, THAT YE ONLY WANT TO!
SIR, I'LL THANK YOU T' KNOW THAT I'M NOT A PURSUIN' WOMAN! WHEN I'M OF MARRYIN' AGE, I'LL GIVE MY HAND AFTER I'VE BEEN PROPERLY COURTED!
NOW AIN'T THAT SENTIMENTAL? HI RECKON YER A RIGHT SMART CHICK! HIT WARMS OL' BLAZE'S VITALS T' 'EAR SUCH SPUNKY TALK...
...BUT HI'M THINKIN' IT'D BE RIGHT SMART FER YE T' LET THEM SWABS THINK YOU TWO IS SPLICED... Y'SEE, THERE WON'T BE NO ROOSTERS STRUTTIN' 'ROUND YOU IF THEY KNOW THEY'LL 'AVE T'ANSWER T' OL' MAN MUSCLES 'ERE!
I RECKON THAT'S MIGHTY WISE, SIR! IT'S SO COMFORTIN' T' KNOW I'LL HAVE A REAL PROTECTOR!
Reg. U. S. Pat. Off.; Copyright, 1939, by News Syndicate Co., Inc.
MILTON CANIFF

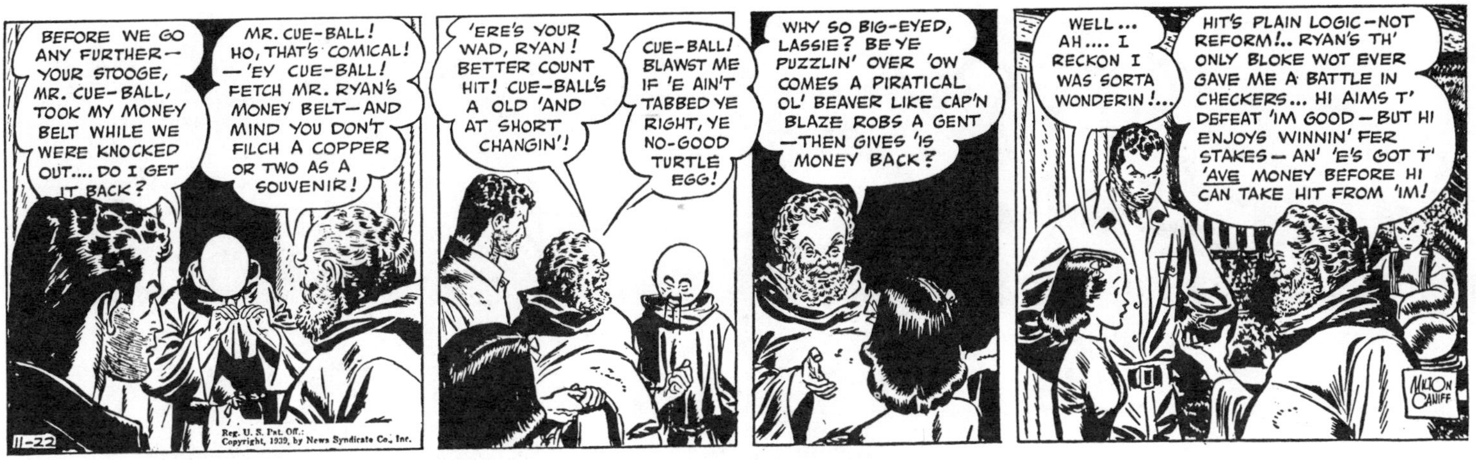
BEFORE WE GO ANY FURTHER— YOUR STOOGE, MR. CUE-BALL, TOOK MY MONEY BELT WHILE WE WERE KNOCKED OUT.... DO I GET IT BACK?
MR. CUE-BALL! HO, THAT'S COMICAL! —'EY CUE-BALL! FETCH MR. RYAN'S MONEY BELT—AND MIND YOU DON'T FILCH A COPPER OR TWO AS A SOUVENIR!
'ERE'S YOUR WAD, RYAN! BETTER COUNT HIT! CUE-BALL'S A OLD 'AND AT SHORT CHANGIN'!
CUE-BALL! BLAWST ME IF 'E AIN'T TABBED YE RIGHT, YE NO-GOOD TURTLE EGG!
WHY SO BIG-EYED, LASSIE? BE YE PUZZLIN' OVER 'OW COMES A PIRATICAL OL' BEAVER LIKE CAP'N BLAZE ROBS A GENT —THEN GIVES 'IS MONEY BACK?
WELL... AH.... I RECKON I WAS SORTA WONDERIN!...
HIT'S PLAIN LOGIC—NOT REFORM!.. RYAN'S TH' ONLY BLOKE WOT EVER GAVE ME A BATTLE IN CHECKERS... HI AIMS T' DEFEAT 'IM GOOD—BUT HI ENJOYS WINNIN' FER STAKES—AN' 'E'S GOT T' 'AVE MONEY BEFORE HI CAN TAKE HIT FROM 'IM!
MILTON CANIFF
11-22
Reg. U. S. Pat. Off.: Copyright, 1939, by News Syndicate Co., Inc.

—BUT WHAT'S ALL THIS GRAND EYEYAM STUFF, CAP'N BLAZE?
HOYO! AIN'T THAT COMICAL? WHEN I STARTED THIS 'ERE HENTERPRISE, HI THINKS HI'D BEST 'AVE A TITLE T' AWE TH' BLOKES...
... I THINKS, HI'M TH' 'EAD MAN 'ERE —SO WHY NOT CALL MESELF TH' GRAND EYEYAM? —AN' TH' STUPID SWABS GOBBLED HIT UP!
BUT, MR. BLAZE—JUS' WHAT IS THIS PLACE?
APRIL-
Y'SEE, MISS, YER PROTECTOR'S SMACK ON TH' JOB! 'E KNOWS OL' BLAZE IS UP T' SOME EVIL—AN' 'E MEANS T' SHIELD YE FROM DANGEROUS KNOWLEDGE...
... IN CHINA, IT AIN'T CUSTOMARY FOR LASSIES T' KNOW MEN'S BUSINESS! S'PPOSE YOU 'OPS ALONG AN' CHANGES THEM THERE PANTALOONS FER SOMETHIN MORE FETCHIN'! THIS BOY'LL STEER YE! STEP ALIVE NOW!
MILTON CANIFF
11-23
Reg. U. S. Pat. Off.: Copyright, 1939, by News Syndicate Co., Inc.

HA HO! YER LITTLE BEAUTY IS TH' PERKY ONE! SHE WUZ THAT PUT OUT WHEN HI ORDERED 'ER T' GO CHANGE 'ER CLOTHES AN' LEAVE US ALONE!
APRIL'S... AH... RATHER PARTIAL TO GIVING THE COMMANDS!
WELL, NOW THAT TH' WEE MISS IS... 'EY! WOT'S ALL TH' ACTIVITY?
LOOKS LIKE A FIRE... ALL THOSE MEN CARRYING WATER!
CUE-BALL! WHO CALLED OUT THEM MEN T' LUG WATER?
MOST AMAZING, SIRE! THE SMALL MISS WALKED UP TO THE GUARDS AND SAID SHE MUST HAVE BATH! ..SHE SMILED UPON EACH IN TURN—ASKED WHO WAS STRONGEST WATER CARRIER AMONG THEM —TWO WERE TRAMPLED IN THE RESULTING STAMPEDE!
... HMM... REGARDLESS OF RACE, COLOR OR PREVIOUS CONDITION OF SERVITUDE...
MILTON CANIFF
11-24
Reg. U. S. Pat. Off.: Copyright, 1939, by News Syndicate Co., Inc.

I THINK YOU BOYS ARE JUS' TOO SWEET T' LI'L OL' ME! YOU'RE ALL SO STRONG! THAT WATER WAS DARLIN'!
MASTER SAY MISSY WEAR PLETTY DLESS! PLEASE TO SELECT!
OH, I DO DECLARE! THEY'RE ALL SO BEAUTIFUL! THAT ONE SHOULD FIT ME RIGHT SMART!
IS DONE!
BLESS ME, THIS IS A REAL PRETTY GOWN... BUT I SEE NO WOMEN ABOUT— TO WHOM AM I INDEBTED FOR LENDING ME HER CLOTHES?
... IS NO PERSON! WOMENS WHO WORE SAME ALL SOLD AS SLAVES TO DESERT CHIEFS! —NO NEED SILK DLESSES SOME MORE! MAKE VELLY SIMPLE — NO?
MILTON CANIFF
11-25
Reg. U. S. Pat. Off.: Copyright, 1939, by News Syndicate Co., Inc.

TERRY AND THE PIRATES
by MILTON CANIFF
Reg. U. S. Pat. Off.: Copyright, 1939, by News Syndicate Co., Inc.
NOW THEN, A BREAK IN THE CYCLE OF EVENTS! THE WHITE GIANT IS A FRIEND OF THE GRAND EYEYAM!
AH, THERE, NO MAN IS REALLY A FRIEND OF THE FIERY ONE!
WELL, HIT'S A SIGHT INDEED T' EYE TH' SECOND BEST CHECKER PLAYER IN CHINA! HI SENT YER LASSIE OFF T' GIT INTO SOME FEMININE FINERY SUCH AS IS PROPER FER WEE WENCHES!
APRIL WILL LIKE THAT!... BUT WHAT'S ALL THIS ODD SETUP, WITH ARMED MONK-LIKE STOOGES AROUND? OPEN UP, BLAZE, YOU OLD SINNER!
IS SOME WRONG? MISSY MEBBE NO LIKE DLESS?
MERCY, NO... IT'S DARLIN'— BUT... BUT... YOU SAID IT BELONGED TO A GIRL WHO WAS SOLD AS A SLAVE TO A DESERT CHIEF! IS...IS THAT WHY THERE ARE NO WOMEN 'ROUND HERE?
OH, MISSY NO WORRY... SHE WIFE OF BIG FRIEND OF MASTER GLAND EYEYAM! NO SELL WIFE OF SAME! NOT HOSPITALITY!
OH.... THIS IS WHY THAT CAP'N BLAZE MAN, OR GRAND EYEYAM, OR WHOEVER HE IS, SAID TO KEEP HIS MEN THINKIN' I AM PAT'S WIFE! BUT HE KNOWS I'M NOT MARRIED! OHHHHH!!!
....SO, AFTER TH' LAST TIME HI SAW YOU AN' YER YOUNG FRIEND, TERRY, HI 'AD BLINKIN' BAD GOIN'... HI THOUGHT OL' CAP'N BLAZE WUZ SLIPPIN' AS A FIRST RATE FREEBOOTER...
...THEN ALONG COMES THIS 'ERE WAR AN' HI KNOWS ME PLUSH DAYS 'AD JUS' BEGUN! THERE AIN'T NO TIME LIKE A WAR FER A GOOD, SLICK SCOUNDREL LIKE ME T' PILE UP TH' PILFER!...
...'ERE, TRY YER 'AND AT TH' DARTS... HIMPROVES YER SHOOTIN' EYE...
... AS HI WUZ SAYIN'.... IN TIMES O' STRIFE YE KIN 'EAR TH' TINGLE O' GOLD, YELLIN' T' BE SPENT— AN' BLAZE AIN'T ONE TO BOTCH ANY BOODLE! HI SET OUT T' TAP TH' TILL O' BOTH ARMIES — AN' RIGHT GOOD HI DID IT... TYKE ME WORD!
PRETTY DANGEROUS, PLAYING BOTH SIDES! ISN'T THERE A CHANCE OF SOMEONE GIVING YOU AWAY?
BLIGH' ME, YES!... IF HI WASN'T TOO SMART FER 'EM! ... FER INSTANCE...
AVAST, YE BILGE RAT! WHEN YE AIMS T' EAVESDROP ON CAP'N BLAZE, NEVER STAND BEHIND A CURTAIN THAT'S SO SHORT YER BIG FEET SHOW! SHOVE OFF!
11-26
LOOKIT OL' CUE-BALL SCAMPER! HI LET'S 'EM 'AVE THEIR FUN SPYIN' —'CAUSE LIFE'S MONOTONOUS 'ERE! — BUT THEY'LL NEVER TRAP BLAZE BY THEM TRICKS! YOU NOTICE YOU GOT NO HINFORMATION — EVEN BY POLITE PRYIN', JUS' NOW! .... WHICH IS A 'INT — SPELLED WITH A CAPITAL HAITCH!

I GATHER WE'RE TO ASK NO QUESTIONS ABOUT YOUR... AH... BUSINESS HERE, 'EH, CAP'N BLAZE?
HO! NOW THAT AIN'T HIT! Y'CAN AWSK ALL YE LIKE... I JUS' DON'T GUARANTEE T' ANSWER! HAWHAW!!
11-27
Reg. U. S. Pat. Off.; Copyright, 1939, by News Syndicate Co., Inc.
WELL, YOU'RE PULLING SOMETHING TO MAKE PROFIT FROM BOTH SIDES IN THE WAR... AND WHAT WE SEE MAY HURT US!
NOW, THAT'S A BLAWSTED SENSIBLE CONCLUSION, RYAN, ME LAD!
WHAT HAPPENS IF WE DO SEE SOMETHING WE'RE NOT SUPPOSED TO?
I'M THINKIN' YE'LL NEED A CHANGE O' DUDS. THERE'S A SHIRT LEFT BY A MAN WOT STOPPED BY 'ERE ONCE! HIT'S BEEN SCRUBBED— AN' TH' BULLET 'OLE'S MENDED...
I GET YOU!
MILTON CANIFF

...HI'M OFF T' ME EVIL PRACTICES! YE'LL FIND SOAP 'AN' SUCH 'ANDY! FITTEN YERSELF UP! TWIDDLE-WIT, 'ERE, WILL SHOW YE YER QUARTERS!
TWIDDLE-WIT IS ME!
OKAY! THANKS, BLAZE!
11-28
Reg. U. S. Pat. Off.; Copyright, 1939, by News Syndicate Co., Inc.
THERE! I FEEL BETTER!
IS FINE! IS MUCH HAN'SOME! FIRS' CLASS! NUMBER ONE! BIG NICE! VELLY...
...IT CAN'T BE THAT GOOD! YOU SHOW ME WHERE I BUNK WHILE YOU'RE THINKING UP A FEW MORE BOUQUETS!
FOLLOW IMMEDIATE CLOSE BEHIND IN STRAIGHT LINE, PLEASE!
OH!
IF MISTER OR WIFE WANT TWIDDLE-WIT, THEY MERELY TO CALL— ME SLEEP OUTSIDE DOOR! GOOD NIGHTS, PLEASE!
MILTON CANIFF

OH, MISTER RYAN—THEY THINK WE'RE MARRIED—SO THEY PUT US IN THE SAME ROOM!
WONDER IF THIS IS CAP'N BLAZE'S IDEA OF A JOKE? ...WORRIED, KITTEN?
11-29
Reg. U. S. Pat. Off.; Copyright, 1939, by News Syndicate Co., Inc.
WELL—AH—NO —ONLY—YOU SEE— I—AH—SORTA...
FOR ONCE IN YOUR LIFE YOU DON'T KNOW THE ANSWERS! REST YOUR MIND—AND STOP BLUSHING... I THINK WE CAN SOLVE THE PROBLEM!
THESE CURTAIN ROPES STRETCHED ACROSS THE ROOM AND COVERED WITH DRAPES WILL DIVIDE THE PLACE PRETTY WELL! YOU'LL HAVE PLENTY OF PRIVACY!
OH, I SAW A MOVIE ONCE WHERE THEY DID THAT!
THEY STRETCHED A BLANKET ACROSS A TOURIST CABIN— THE MAN CALLED IT "THE WALLS OF JERICHO!"
LOOK CLOSELY, SUGAH! YOU'LL OBSERVE THAT I HAVEN'T A SINGLE TRUMPET CONCEALED ABOUT ME— ANYWHERE!

I'M GOING TO PUT OUT THE LIGHT APRIL— READY?
UH HUH!
11-30
MISTER RYAN, I THINK YOU'RE MIGHTY NICE T' BE SO GALLANT ABOUT ALL THIS!
THANK YOU, KITTEN! GLAD YOU THINK SO!
THERE AREN'T MANY MEN A GIRL COULD FEEL SO SECURE WITH! IT'S MOS' REASSURIN'!
DON'T MENTION IT, SUGAH! GOOD NIGHT!
MILTON CANIFF
Reg. U. S. Pat. Off.; Copyright, 1939, by News Syndicate Co., Inc.

12-1
HEY!
DID MISTER MAKE CALL, PLEASE?
...IT'S NOTHING! MUST HAVE BEEN DREAMING... BUT I'D SWEAR SOMETHING WARM TOUCHED MY LIPS! .... FUNNY!
MILTON CANIFF
Reg. U. S. Pat. Off.; Copyright, 1939, by News Syndicate Co., Inc.

...CAN'T GET BACK TO SLEEP... GLAD I DIDN'T WAKEN APRIL BY YELLING LIKE A KID AFRAID OF THE DARK... WISH I KNEW HOW TERRY AND THE GANG ARE MAKING OUT...
12-2
...WE'RE NOT IN CLOVER OURSELVES... OLD BLAZE IS UP TO SOME HIGH DEVILTRY! —WISH I KNEW WHAT... WE'RE NOT SAFE HERE BY ANY MEANS!... HEY! I HEAR MOTORS... TRUCKS RUMBLING...
...HMM... LOADING INVADER LORRIES WITH BULKY PACKAGES ...DOESN'T LOOK LIKE FOOD OR GUNS... THIS MUST BE HALF OF BLAZE'S ENTERPRISE TO PROFIT FROM BOTH SIDES IN THE WAR...
...IF WE COULD GET SOMETHING ON THE OLD REPROBATE WE MIGHT SLICKER OUR WAY OUT OF HERE... THE INVADER WOULDN'T GET SUPPLIES IN THIS OUT OF THE WAY PLACE... BUT HE MIGHT GET.... I WONDER....
MILTON CANIFF
Reg. U. S. Pat. Off.; Copyright, 1939, by News Syndicate Co., Inc.

TERRY AND THE PIRATES
by MILTON CANIFF
WHAT'S AILIN' YOU, MISTER RYAN? I DECLARE, I NEVER SAW YOU IN SUCH A FIDGET!
NO USE DODGING THE ISSUE, APRIL, WE'RE IN A PECULIAR SPOT! THIS CAP'N BLAZE IS A THOROUGH VILLAIN — IN SPITE OF HIS WARM WELCOME TO US!
I KNOW! THIS NICE DRESS ONCE BELONGED TO A GIRL HE SOLD AS A SLAVE!
... AND THESE CLOTHES HE GAVE ME WERE ONCE WORN BY A PREVIOUS VISITOR—WHO EVIDENTLY WAS SHOT FOR KNOWING TOO MUCH! WE'RE SEMI-PRISONERS HERE, THOUGH WE'RE WELL TREATED...
...AN' WE JUS' CAN'T GET AWAY WHEN WE WISH TO —'CAUSE TH' COUNTRY'S A MESS FROM THE RAINS!
DANGEROUS AS IT IS TO KNOW BLAZE'S BUSINESS, I THINK OUR ONLY WAY OUT IS TO GET SOMETHING ON HIM — BECAUSE HE'S MAKING PROFITS FROM BOTH ARMIES! ... JUST LAST NIGHT A FLEET OF INVADER TRUCKS LOADED UP HERE... I SAW THEM FROM THE WINDOW...
...AN' YOU AIM TO LEARN WHAT IT WAS THEY HAULED AWAY!...
I HAVE A FAINT HUNCH... VERY FAINT... BUT I'VE GOT TO BE SURE! YOU CAN HELP ME, IF YOU WILL! IT WILL TAKE A BIT OF ACTING...
GREAT DAY! I RECKON I'M TH' WORLD'S WORST ACTRESS, BUT I'M SURE NUFF WILLIN' T' TRY! WHAT'S TH' PLOT?

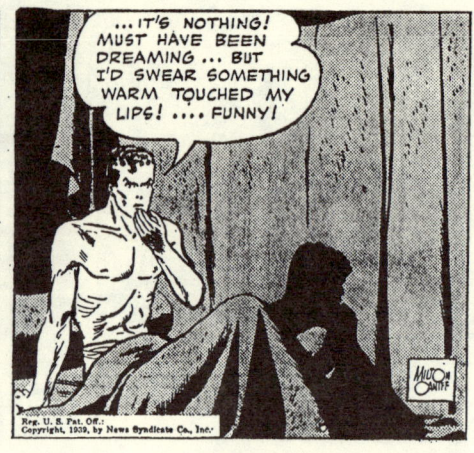

LATER
WELL, BLOW ME TOPPER! IF HIT AIN'T TH' WEE LASS — DRESSED ALL PROPER! 'EY, WHY SO DROOPY, MISS?
OH, H'LLO! I DUNNO, MISTER BLAZE... RECKON TH' RAIN'S MADE ME GLOOMY! I'M SORTA HOMESICK AN' BLUE!
'ERE, RYAN! WOT SORT OF AN ESCORT ARE YE? YER LASSIE'S IN TH' DUMPS, FER SURE! WHERE'S YER WELL-KNOWN KNACK FER CHARMIN' TH' LADIES?
TH' KID DEFEATS ME, CAP'N BLAZE! I THINK SHE MISSES THE THINGS SHE WAS USED TO AT HOME... YOU KNOW, PLENTY OF FLOWERS AND...
FLOWERS? WHY, BLIGH' ME, NEVER LET HIT BE SAID THAT CAP'N BLAZE EVER DISAPPOINTED A MISS WHO FANCIED POSIES! 'EY, CUE-BALL, SHAKE A LEG AN' FETCH SOME BLOOMS!
BUT AT ONCE, MASTER!
'ERE YE BE! HI RECKON BLAZE AIN'T ONE T' ALLOW A PRETTY T' PINE FER WANT OF A FLOCK O' BLOSSOMS!
OH, CAP'N BLAZE, THIS IS WONDERFUL! JUST LOOK! LOTS AN' LOTS OF POPPIES!
12-3
LOTS AND LOTS OF POPPIES! WE GUESSED RIGHT! POPPIES CAN MEAN ONLY ONE THING— THE OLD BOY'S WHOLESALING OPIUM!!
Reg. U. S. Pat. Off. Copyright, 1939, by News Syndicate Co., Inc.
OH, CAP'N BLAZE, I THINK IT WAS JUS' DOWNRIGHT CHARMIN' OF YOU T' HAVE THESE LOVELY POPPIES BROUGHT IN FOR ME! IT NEARLY SETS ME T'SWOONIN'!
YER WELCOME, MISSY! BY TH' BY, DO YE — AH — KNOW ANYTHIN' ABOUT POPPIES?
12-4
ONLY THAT THEY'RE BEAUTIFUL! I RECKON THAT'S ALL THAT MATTERS, ISN'T IT?
HMM... RIGHT YE BE, LASS! WELL, SINCE ME POSIES FIXED YER FIT O' GLOOMIN', I'LL BE ABOUT ME AFFAIRS! CHEER'O!
I DECLARE, MISTER RYAN, YOUR HUNCH WAS CORRECT! WHEN I PLAY-ACTED LIKE I WAS LONESOME FOR TH' FLOWERS BACK HOME, HE BROUGHT ME POPPIES! THAT MEANS CAP'N BLAZE IS PROBABLY MAKIN' OPIUM!
SHHH!
OH, BEG PARDON! CLUMSY OF ME! ...THOUGHT YOU HAD GONE, CAP'N!
HI JUST POPPED BACK LOOKIN' FER ME WITS — WHICH HI MUST 'AVE MISLAID WHEN YOU TWO 'APPENED IN 'ERE!
MILTON CANIFF
Reg. U. S. Pat. Off.; Copyright, 1939, by News Syndicate Co., Inc.
'OW NOW, LASS, WHY DON'T YE SKIP T' YER ROOM AN' PARCEL OUT YER POSIES? ME AN' RYAN 'AVE THINGS T' DISCUSS!
OH — ALL RIGHT!
12-5
WELL, YE DONE HIT, YE SMART ROGUE! HI'VE 'ALF A MIND T' LOP OFF THAT BLAWSTED 'EAD OF YOURS!
WHY, CAPTAIN, YOU TALK LIKE HENRY THE EIGHTH! HERE I STAND JUST DRIPPING WITH INNOCENCE — AND YOU WANT TO SLICE ME UP!
Reg. U. S. Pat. Off.; Copyright, 1939, by News Syndicate Co., Inc.
INNOCENCE, ME EYE! YE COOKED UP THAT GLOOM O' TH' LASSIE'S SO'S HI'D FETCH 'ER FLOWERS — AN' WHEN YE SAW THEY WUZ POPPIES — YE GUESSED HI WUZ MAKIN' OPIUM!
MILTON CANIFF
WELL, WHAT HAPPENS? DO I GET WIPED OUT BECAUSE I KNOW TOO MUCH?
YE KNOW BLOOMIN' WELL HI WON'T SHOOT YE DOWN — 'CAUSE YER TH' ONLY BLOKE WOT KIN GIVE ME A BATTLE AT DRAUGHTS! SETTLE YERSELF AN' SHUT UP!

YOU'RE SUNK, CAP'N BLAZE! THAT'S TWO OUT OF THREE FOR ME!
CURSE YE FER A KNAVE, RYAN! WE'LL PLAY BEST THREE OUT O' FIVE! HI'LL 'AVE YER 'IDE YET!
12-6
Reg. U. S. Pat. Off.; Copyright, 1939, by News Syndicate Co., Inc.
MILTON CANIFF
I ... AH ... BEG PARDON, I DON'T BELIEVE I'VE HAD THE PLEASURE OF MEETING THIS YOUNG LADY!
OH, 'ER? SHE'S ME DAUGHTER — AN' WE AIN'T SPEAKIN'! YER MOVE, RYAN!

BLOATED SPECTACLE OF DECADENCE THAT IS BY EVIL CHANCE MY FATHER! I LOOK UPON YOU WITH CONTEMPT!
RYAN, WILL YOU TELL 'ER T' GO AWAY? HI AIN'T SPEAKIN' T' TH' WINDY WENCH!
12-7
Reg. U. S. Pat. Off.; Copyright, 1939, by News Syndicate Co., Inc.
AFTER ALL, BLAZE, IF SHE'S YOUR DAUGHTER I DON'T FEEL IT'S MY PLACE ....
WELL SPOKEN! HIS WEAK BRAIN HASN'T THE STRENGTH OR DEPTH TO OVERCOME MY MENTAL SUPERIORITY! THUS HE APPEALS TO A STRANGER!
RYAN, WILL YE DO A OL' PAL A FAVOR AN' PAY NO ATTENTION TO 'ER BLATHERIN'? YE GETS USED TO HIT AFTER AWHILE! IN TIME THEM BIG WORDS SOUNDS LIKE TH' STEADY MURMUR OF A BROOK!
HE IS TOO GREAT A FOOL TO EVEN BE DISTURBED BY THE ACID OF MY SPEECH! THE FAT OF HIS BODY HAS EXTENDED TO HIS BRAIN! CEREBRAL CORPULENCE!
THIS IS EMBARRASSING! YOU MIGHT TELL ME THE YOUNG LADY'S NAME — SO I CAN SPEAK TO HER!
HER NAME IS CHEERY! ... CHEERY BLAZE! ... AN' HI ONCE THOUGHT THAT WUZ QUAINT!!
MILTON CANIFF

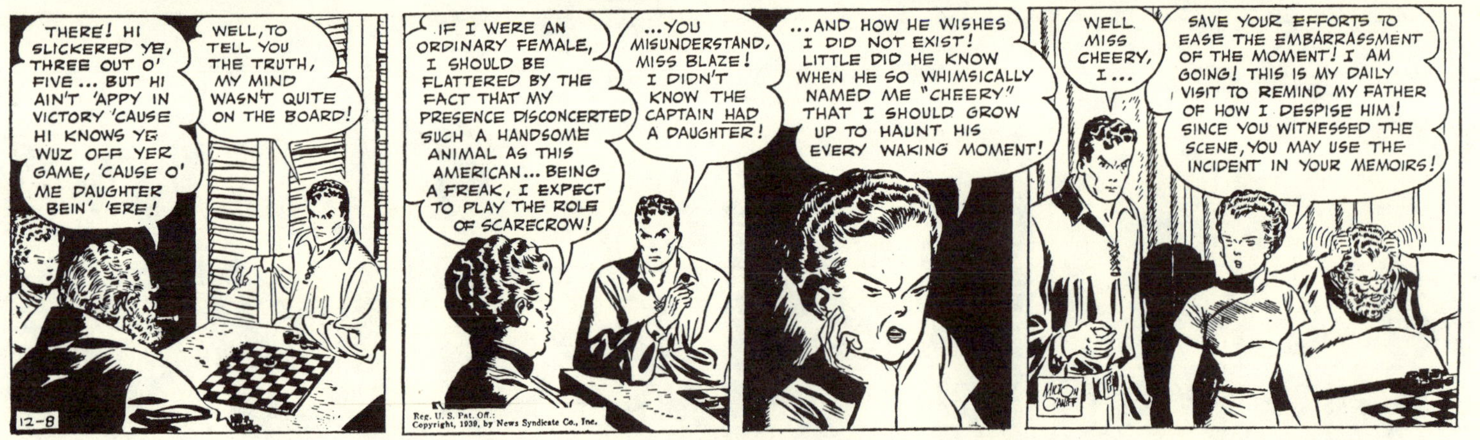
THERE! HI SLICKERED YE, THREE OUT O' FIVE ... BUT HI AIN'T 'APPY IN VICTORY 'CAUSE HI KNOWS YE WUZ OFF YER GAME, 'CAUSE O' ME DAUGHTER BEIN' 'ERE!
WELL, TO TELL YOU THE TRUTH, MY MIND WASN'T QUITE ON THE BOARD!
12-8
IF I WERE AN ORDINARY FEMALE, I SHOULD BE FLATTERED BY THE FACT THAT MY PRESENCE DISCONCERTED SUCH A HANDSOME ANIMAL AS THIS AMERICAN ... BEING A FREAK, I EXPECT TO PLAY THE ROLE OF SCARECROW!
... YOU MISUNDERSTAND, MISS BLAZE! I DIDN'T KNOW THE CAPTAIN HAD A DAUGHTER!
Reg. U. S. Pat. Off.; Copyright, 1939, by News Syndicate Co., Inc.
... AND HOW HE WISHES I DID NOT EXIST! LITTLE DID HE KNOW WHEN HE SO WHIMSICALLY NAMED ME "CHEERY" THAT I SHOULD GROW UP TO HAUNT HIS EVERY WAKING MOMENT!
WELL, MISS CHEERY, I ...
SAVE YOUR EFFORTS TO EASE THE EMBARRASSMENT OF THE MOMENT! I AM GOING! THIS IS MY DAILY VISIT TO REMIND MY FATHER OF HOW I DESPISE HIM! SINCE YOU WITNESSED THE SCENE, YOU MAY USE THE INCIDENT IN YOUR MEMOIRS!
MILTON CANIFF

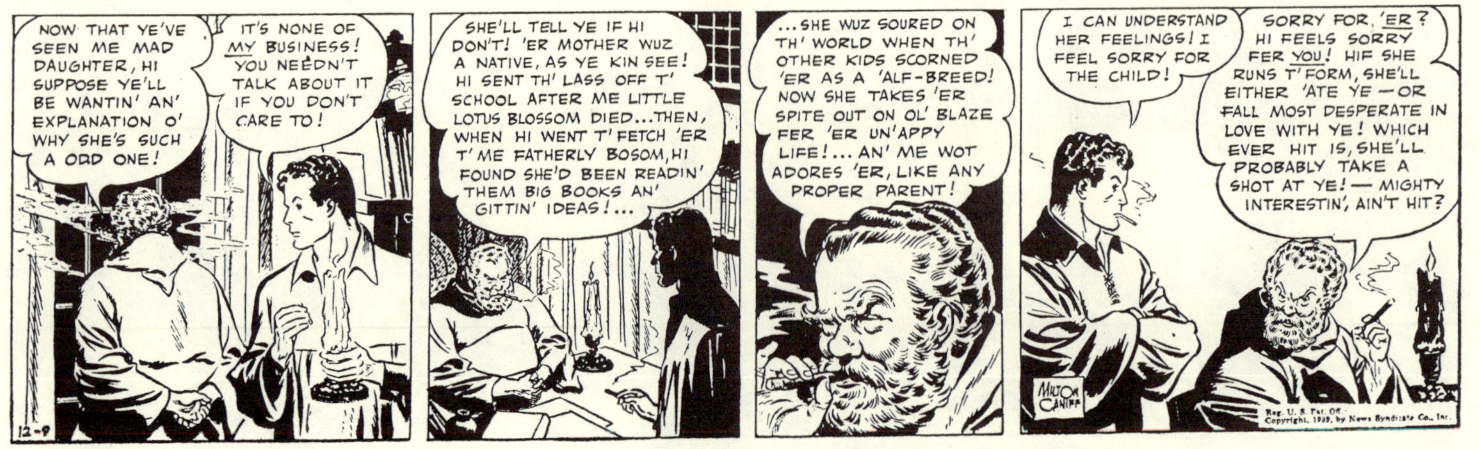
NOW THAT YE'VE SEEN ME MAD DAUGHTER, HI SUPPOSE YE'LL BE WANTIN' AN' EXPLANATION O' WHY SHE'S SUCH A ODD ONE!
IT'S NONE OF MY BUSINESS! YOU NEEDN'T TALK ABOUT IT IF YOU DON'T CARE TO!
12-9
SHE'LL TELL YE IF HI DON'T! 'ER MOTHER WUZ A NATIVE, AS YE KIN SEE! HI SENT TH' LASS OFF T' SCHOOL AFTER ME LITTLE LOTUS BLOSSOM DIED ... THEN, WHEN HI WENT T' FETCH 'ER T' ME FATHERLY BOSOM, HI FOUND SHE'D BEEN READIN' THEM BIG BOOKS AN' GITTIN' IDEAS! ...
... SHE WUZ SOURED ON TH' WORLD WHEN TH' OTHER KIDS SCORNED 'ER AS A 'ALF-BREED! NOW SHE TAKES 'ER SPITE OUT ON OL' BLAZE FER 'ER UN'APPY LIFE! ... AN' ME WOT ADORES 'ER, LIKE ANY PROPER PARENT!
I CAN UNDERSTAND HER FEELINGS! I FEEL SORRY FOR THE CHILD!
SORRY FOR 'ER? HI FEELS SORRY FER YOU! HIF SHE RUNS T' FORM, SHE'LL EITHER 'ATE YE — OR FALL MOST DESPERATE IN LOVE WITH YE! WHICH EVER HIT IS, SHE'LL PROBABLY TAKE A SHOT AT YE! — MIGHTY INTERESTIN', AIN'T HIT?
MILTON CANIFF
Reg. U. S. Pat. Off.; Copyright, 1939, by News Syndicate Co., Inc.

TERRY AND THE PIRATES
by MILTON CANIFF
I DO DECLARE! SUCH INTRIGUE I NEVER DID SEE! MISTER RYAN KNEW WHEN THOSE POPPIES WERE BROUGHT IN THAT THIS CAP'N BLAZE WAS PROBABLY MAKIN' OPIUM!
HE SAYS THE INVADERS GIVE THE DRUG TO TH' POOR CHINESE PEOPLE T' KEEP 'EM QUIET! IT'S WAR WITHOUT GUNS!
SUN'S OUT! MISTER RYAN AN' CAP'N BLAZE ARE OFF GABBIN' SOMEWHERE ...THINK I'LL TAKE A WALK OUT O' THIS SPOOKY HOUSE! I'M A LITTLE MITE SCARED!
I SWEAR T' GOODNESS I ACHED FOR ADVENTURE AN' SUCH — AN' I'M SURE NUFF GETTIN' IT IN GREAT BATCHES ... OH! WHAT'S THAT?
PARASITE!!
GLORY BE! YOU FRIGHTENED ME HALF TO DEATH! I DON'T RIGHTLY KNOW WHAT I'VE DONE T' CAUSE YOU T' SHOUT NAMES AT ME... BUT I DEEPLY APOLOGIZE IF I'VE OFFENDED IN ANY WAY!
HA! IT IS NOT WHAT YOU'VE DONE ... IT IS THAT YOU DO NOTHING!! YOU LEAN UPON THE HANDSOME AMERICAN LIKE ALL WOMEN OF YOUR KIND! BARNACLE! LEECH! I'VE BEEN WATCHING!
FRANKLY, MISS, I'M MOST BOWLED OVER BY ALL THIS... BUT I RECKON YOU HAVE A PERFECT RIGHT TO YOUR OPINION!
THAT'S CHARACTERISTIC! YOU HAVEN'T THE STRENGTH OF WILL TO FIGHT BACK WHEN I CONFRONT YOU WITH THE TRUTH! SPINELESS CREATURE, WHO MUST BUY PROTECTION FROM SOME MALE BY WILES AND BEAUTY! I DESPISE YOU!
OH, DEAR, THAT JUS' GRIEVES ME TO TH' BONE...
... IT'D BE RIGHT NICE T' HAVE A GIRL FRIEND NEAR MY OWN AGE HERE IN THIS LONELY PLACE! ...BUT O' COURSE, IF YOU DISLIKE ME SO MUCH, I RECKON MY COMPANY WOULD FRET YOU!
YOU'LL HAVE PLENTY OF COMPANY! ALREADY ALL THE MEN HERE ARE ANXIOUS TO DO YOUR BIDDING! EVEN MY FATHER, CAP'N BLAZE, SEES IN YOU WHAT HE WISHES I HAD BEEN!
BLESS ME! I DIDN'T RIGHTLY KNOW MISTER BLAZE HAD A DAUGHTER.... BUT COME...
... BUT COME TO THINK OF IT, I DO RESEMBLE HIM, DO I NOT? SAME HAIR! SAME FIGURE, BEFORE LONG! A GROSS CREATURE- A CARICATURE! A RED-HEADED SCARECROW WITH SLANT-EYES!...
... BUT ONE THING CANNOT BE DENIED ME... I HAVE THE SPIRIT OF THE WESTERN RACES, PLUS THE CUNNING OF THE CHINESE! I AM WISER THAN ANY OF YOU! I AM SUPERIOR, DO YOU HEAR? —SUPERIOR!!
I – I'M MOS' DELIGHTED TO KNOW THAT, MISS... MISS....
12-10
CHEERY!... CHEERY BLAZE, MY FATHER NAMED ME! WHICH IS THE CROWNING IRONY! GO ON! YOU DO NOT HAVE TO WAIT UNTIL I HAVE DEPARTED TO START TO LAUGH! IN FACT I WILL JOIN YOU ...HAHAHAHA!!!

OH, MR. RYAN, I JUST MET TH' MOST PITIFUL GIRL ...
REALLY? IT MUST HAVE BEEN CHEERY BLAZE, THE CAP'N'S DAUGHTER ...
WHY, YES! HOW DID YOU KNOW?
A PRETTY GIRL ONLY USES THE WORD "PITIFUL" ABOUT A LESS ATTRACTIVE ONE ... AND CHEERY'S NO ORCHID!
OH, YOU CAN BE MADDENIN' MEAN SOMETIMES ... SAYIN' SUCH THINGS!
WELL, IT'S TRUE, ISN'T IT? YOU CAN BE PATRONIZING TO HER — SINCE YOU MAKE HER LOOK LIKE A TUMBLEWEED PLACED NEXT TO A MAGNOLIA BLOSSOM!
I SHOULD SNOOT YOU FOR MAKIN' ME OUT UPPITY .... BUT IT WAS SWEET OF YOU TO SAY SUCH NICE THINGS 'BOUT OL' ME!
12-11
Reg. U. S. Pat. Off.: Copyright, 1939, by News Syndicate Co., Inc.
MILTON CANIFF

THAT WAS A MOS' DELICIOUS DINNER, CAP'N BLAZE ... I WAS JUS' WONDERIN' WHY MISS CHEERY ISN'T WITH US!
HO, LASS! SO YE'VE MET ME CONTRARY OFFSPRING, TOO! ... WELL, NO NEED T' PLAY-ACT ABOUT HIT ...
... ME DAUGHTER WILL 'AVE NONE O' ME TABLE! SHE 'ATES ME POISONOUS ... SHE SUPS IN 'ER OWN DIGGIN'S — WHICH IRKS ME DREADFUL!
OH, THAT'S REAL DISTRESSIN'! IF Y'ALL WILL EXCUSE ME, I'LL GO MAKE MY MANNERS TO HER!
IF MISSY FOLLOW CLOSE BEHIND IN STRAIGHT LINE, TWIDDLE-WIT SHOW EXACTLY SPOT WHERE MISSY RED-TOP MAKE EATINGS!
IS LITTLE MISSY BLACK-TOP COME MAKE HOW-DO TO MISSY RED-TOP FOR SOCIABLE PURPOSE!
TELL HER TO GO AWAY AND ADMIRE HERSELF IN PRIVATE!
12-12
Reg. U. S. Pat. Off. Copyright, 1939, by News Syndicate Co., Inc.
MILTON CANIFF

TELL THAT DELICATE AND WELL-NURTURED FLOWER I DO NOT WISH TO ENDURE HER FRAGRANCE!
AH ... IS CLEAR MISSY IS ADMIRED, BUT ONLY AT DISTANCE!
YOU JUS' SKIP ON, TWIDDLE-WIT! I'LL SORTA PASS TH' TIME O' DAY!
I DON'T MEAN T' PRESUME ON YOUR PRIVACY, MISS CHEERY, BUT I'VE BEEN RIGHT LONELY ... AN' I THOUGHT YOU MIGHT CHAT WITH ME A MITE!
HOW ABSURD ... WITH YOUR HANDSOME AMERICAN AND EVERY OTHER MAN IN THIS PLACE FAWNING AT YOUR FEET!
... YOU CAME TO AMUSE YOURSELF AT MY GROTESQUERIES! WELL, WHY DO YOU NOT LAUGH ALOUD? ... OR DO YOU THINK THAT BEING KIND WILL CAUSE ME TO SUFFER MORE BY CONTRAST?
WHY NOTHIN' LIKE THAT, MISS CHEERY! I THOUGHT IT MIGHT BE COZY T' HAVE A CUP O' TEA WITH YOU! IT'S NICE T' TALK TO ANOTHER GIRL ...
... ESPECIALLY WHEN SHE IS UGLY ENOUGH TO CAUSE YOU TO APPEAR MORE ALLURING! UNFORTUNATE THAT THERE ARE NO MEN TO SEE! HERE'S YOUR TEA ... I REGRET THERE IS NO POISON IN IT!
12-13
1939, by News Syndicate Co., Inc.
MILTON CANIFF

MY, THIS IS REAL COZY, WITH TH' RAIN COMIN' DOWN OUTSIDE! I'LL JUS' BET THOSE BOOKS ARE INTERESTIN'!
OH, INDEED! THEY HAVE SUCH PRETTY COVERS, TOO! THAT WILL BE AS CLOSE AS YOU WILL EVER COME TO THEM!
'COURSE, MISS CHEERY, I COULD NEVER HOPE T' BE AS LEARNED AS YOU ... BUT I'D LOVE T' READ SOME OF 'EM — WHILE WE'RE WAITIN' FOR TH' RAIN T' LET UP SO WE CAN MOVE ON!
I SHOULDN'T THINK YOU WOULD BE ANXIOUS ... WITH YOUR HANDSOME HUSBAND TO KEEP YOU COMPANY HERE!
HUSBAND? OH, GREAT DAY, MR. RYAN AN' I AREN'T MARRIED! THE MEN WHO FOUND US JUS' TOOK THAT FOR GRANTED ... AN' YOUR DADDY SAID IT'D BE BEST IF WE LET 'EM THINK SO! ...
... WHY, MISS CHEERY, WHAT IN TH' WORLD AILS YOU?
12-14
Reg. U. S. Pat. Off.: Copyright, 1939, by News Syndicate Co., Inc.
MILTON CANIFF

FOOL! FOOL! BEAUTIFUL LITTLE FOOL, SO SMUGLY COMPLACENT IN THE POWER OF YOUR DOLL'S FACE! YOU SHALL WISH YOU WERE BORN A DRAB DUCKLING!
I DO DECLARE, MISS CHEERY... I DON'T JUS' SEE WHY MY NOT BEIN' MR. RYAN'S WIFE HAS YOU SO FUSSED UP!
12-15
OF COURSE YOU DON'T... SO I WILL TELL YOU, IF I CAN CONTROL MY LAUGHTER... YOU THINK PERHAPS I WILL SEEK HIS FAVOR, NOW THAT I KNOW HE IS UNMARRIED! I AM NOT SUCH AN OPTIMIST...
...BUT LISTEN TO THIS! MY FATHER, CAP'N BLAZE, DOES BUSINESS WITH A WILD TRIBESMAN FROM THE NORTHERN BORDER COUNTRY NAMED SINGH-SINGH! THIS MAN BRINGS SMUGGLED GUNS AND AMMUNITION TO THIS PLACE, WHICH THE INVADER THINKS IS AN OPIUM FARM...
...BUT I STILL DON'T SEE....
QUIET!—YOU WILL! MY FATHER, IN TURN, SELLS THE ARMS TO THE CHINESE AT A GREAT PROFIT! IN ORDER TO KEEP SINGH-SINGH'S TRADE, MY FATHER MUST REWARD HIM ON EACH TRIP WITH A VERY SPECIAL BONUS! A NEW WIFE FOR HIS HAREM — ONE WHO SPEAKS ENGLISH!
MILTON CANIFF
Reg. U. S. Pat. Off.: Copyright, 1939, by News Syndicate Co., Inc.

OH, MERCY SAVE ME! YOU MEAN THAT IF THIS SINGH-SINGH MAN WANTS A WIFE WHO SPEAKS ENGLISH FOR HIS HAREM EACH TIME HE COMES HERE THAT TH' NEXT ONE WILL BE OL' ME?
OF COURSE! YOUR BEING HELD HERE BY THE RAINS WAS ACCIDENTAL... BUT WHAT A GOLDEN BOON FOR MY FATHER, WHO IS EXPECTING SINGH-SINGH ANY DAY!
12-16
MY FATHER ALLOWED THE MEN TO THINK YOU AND RYAN WERE MARRIED SO ONE OF THEM WOULDN'T KIDNAP YOU AND DESERT—IN ORDER TO SELL YOU DIRECT TO SINGH-SINGH! THE TRIBESMAN WILL NOT ACCEPT GIRLS WHO HAVE BEEN MARRIED TO SOMEONE ELSE!
GREAT DAY! AN' I THOUGHT CAP'N BLAZE WAS BEIN' SO KIND AN' HOSPITABLE! WE'VE JUS' GOT T' LEAVE HERE! I'LL GET MISTER RYAN...
Reg. U. S. Pat. Off.: Copyright, 1939, by News Syndicate Co., Inc.
...TO THE EAST AND SOUTH THE RIVERS ARE FLOODED BY THE RAINS; TO THE NORTH LIES THE INVADER ARMY; TO THE WEST ARE TRACKLESS MILES OF MUD... AND YOU ARE SURROUNDED BY ARMED MEN AND BARBED WIRE! YOU'LL GO WHERE, LITTLE FRIGHTENED DOVE?
MILTON CANIFF

TERRY AND THE PIRATES
by MILTON CANIFF
MISTER RYAN! MISTER RYAN!!
APRIL! WHAT ON EARTH...?
I WENT UP T'HAVE TEA WITH MISS CHEERY BLAZE, AN' HAPPENED T' MENTION THAT WE WEREN'T REALLY MARRIED... SHE SAID THAT'S WHY WE'RE BEIN' ALLOWED T' STAY HERE....
BUT HOW....?
...'CAUSE THERE'S AN AWFUL MAN, NAMED SINGH-SINGH, WHO BRINGS GUNS HERE FOR CAP'N BLAZE T' SELL T' TH' CHINESE! TH' CAP'N MAKES A BIG PROFIT, BUT HE MUST GIVE THIS SINGH-SINGH A BONUS OF A NEW WIFE WHO SPEAKS ENGLISH FOR HIS HAREM EACH TIME HE COMES! TH' NEXT ONE IS ME!
CAP'N BLAZE LET TH' MEN THINK YOU ARE MY HUSBAND — SO ONE OF 'EM WOULDN'T DESERT, KIDNAP ME, AN' CARRY ME OFF T' SINGH-SINGH FOR PRIVATE SALE... THIS TRIBESMAN WON'T TAKE GIRLS WHO'VE BEEN MARRIED!
WELL, BLAZE!
HAHAHA! SUCH PLEASURE IT IS TO SEE THE FAT FOOL FACED WITH HIS QUAINT SCHEME! YOUR RESPECTED CHECKER OPPONENT IS RIGHTEOUSLY INDIGNANT! WHY DO YOU NOT SPEAK UP?
NOW, TAKE HIT EASY, ME BUCKO! YE NEEDN'T ACT LIKE TH' 'ANDSOME 'ERO! HIT'LL GIT YE NO PLACE 'ERE!...

...YER A SENSIBLE BLOKE, IN SPITE O' YER 'OT 'EAD! ONE YIP FROM ME AN' YE'LL BE SHOT DOWN BY ME GUARDS! SO DISENTANGLE THAT LUNCH 'OOK FROM ME GARMENTS AN' I'LL ELABORATE ON ME CHARMIN' DAUGHTER'S TALL TALE!
YOU CAN BE ASSURED THAT THE ROGUE'S EXPLANATION WILL BE FASCINATING! I WILL LEAVE YOU NOW! I AM ALWAYS BORED BY HIS LIES!
YE NEEDN'T BELIEVE THIS —BUT WOT ME UN'APPY DAUGHTER SAYS IS TRUE! HI MUST SUPPLY THIS SKUNK, SINGH-SINGH, WITH AN ENGLISH-SPEAKIN', UNMARRIED LASS EACH TIME 'E BRINGS A LOAD O' GUNS! TH' DIFFERENCE IS, I WUZ NOT INTENDIN' T' SELL THIS COMELY LASS TO TH' EVIL GENT!
..TRUE HIT IS, THAT I'M EXPECTIN' SINGH-SINGH ANY DAY — AN' I AIN'T GOT TH' USUAL ENGLISH-SPEAKIN' NATIVE GIRL HI USUALLY GITS FROM ME CITY CONNECTIONS.... BUT YOU FILLIN' TH' BILL IS PURE ACCIDENT! TH' MEN DUBBED YE MAN AN' WIFE.... AN' TH' RAINS 'OLD YE 'ERE...
...HI SUGGESTED KEEPIN' UP TH' MARRIAGE POSE SO SOME O' ME NO-GOOD 'OODLUMS WOULD THINK TWICE BEFORE RISKIN' THE IRE O' ONE-PUNCH RYAN BY MAKIN' EYES AT TH' WEE LASS!... B'LIEVE ME, HI'VE RACKED ME FEEBLE BRAIN THINKIN' OF A WAY OUT O' ALL THIS...
...BUT ME POOR CHEERY 'AS BROUGHT HIT TO A 'EAD! NOW WE CAN ALL BEND OUR WITS T' TH' PROBLEM! HI'VE THOUGHT O' 'IDIN' YOU TWO—BUT TH' MEN WOULD TELL SINGH-SINGH YE WUZ 'ERE... SO WE'VE GOT T' 'ATCH A BETTER SCHEME!
WELL, BLAZE, YOUR STORY RINGS TRUE! FORTUNATELY, EVERYONE IN YOUR MOB THINKS APRIL'S MY WIFE — THAT'S ONE BREAK WE HAVE!

LASS, I CAN'T BLAME YE FER GITTIN' SCARED... WHEN ME DAUGHTER CHEERY TOLD YE HI WUZ AIMIN' T' SELL YE T' SINGH-SINGH...
12-18
NOR CAN I BLAME YE, RYAN, FER LEAPIN' AT ME THROAT WHEN TH' WEE ONE CAME SOBBIN' T' YE FER PROTECTION... BUT HI'M 'APPY YE BELIEVES ME EXPLANATION!
YES, YOUR STORY MAKES SENSE—THAT APRIL'S ELIGIBILITY AS A WIFE FOR THIS SINGH-SINGH IS JUST A COINCIDENCE....
Reg. U. S. Pat. Off.) Copyright, 1939, by News Syndicate Co., Inc.
BUT WHY IS IT YOU DON'T HAVE THE USUAL UNMARRIED, ENGLISH-SPEAKING NATIVE GIRL YOU ALWAYS FURNISH FOR THIS HILL-BULLY?
HIT JUST SHOWS YE CAN'T TRUST 'UMAN NATURE, SON! HI MADE THE ERROR O' SENDIN' A STRAPPIN' LAD T' FETCH A GAL FROM ME CITY AGENTS! ...ON TH' WAY 'ERE THEY FALLS IN LOVE — AN' ALL HI GOT WUZ A WEDDIN' ANNOUNCEMENT! ...HIT'S TOO LATE FER ANOTHER TRIP!
MILTON CANIFF

BUT MISTER BLAZE, WHY IN TH' WIDE WORLD DOES THIS AWFUL SINGH-SINGH PERSON WANT ALL HIS WIVES T' SPEAK ENGLISH?
THERE'S A ODD THING, LASSIE! OL' SINGH-SINGH ONCE WUZ A WRESTLER...
12-19
...'E BUMMED AROUN' TH' FAR EAST, FIGHTIN' FER FISH AN' CHIPS.... THEN SOMEHOW 'E POPPED UP IN NEW YORK, STOKIN' ON A GREASY FREIGHTER! 'E TURNED T' WRESTLIN' FER EATS — AN' SOME PROMOTER SPOTS 'IM, AN' PRESENTS 'IM AS "SINGH-SINGH, THE EURASIAN ERUPTION"....
A URAL YOKEL, EH? GO ON, BLAZE!
WELL, OL' SINGH SAVED 'IS COPPERS, 'CAUSE 'IS MANAGERS WANTED T' FOSTER THE EURASIAN LEGEND AN' WOULDN'T ALLOW 'IM T' GO OUT ANYWHERE! WHEN 'E'D MADE 'IS PILE, 'E 'AULED ANCHOR AN' CAME 'OME...
'IS WRESTLIN' MONEY WUZ A BIG FORTUNE IN 'IS NATIVE VILLAGE...AN' WITH HIT 'E SET UP 'IS GUN-RUNNIN' BUSINESS... —NOW 'E'S RICH — BUT BECAUSE 'E WUZ KEPT UNDER COVER IN NEW YORK, 'E NEVER LEARNED ENGLISH — TODAY 'E'S EDUCATIN' 'IMSELF BY 'AVIN' NONE BUT ENGLISH-SPEAKIN' WIVES! AIN'T THAT EDIFYIN'?
MILTON CANIFF

SOUNDS AS IF THIS SINGH-SINGH IS QUITE INGENIOUS! BUT WHY IS HE SO ANXIOUS TO SPEAK ENGLISH?
'E THINKS NEW YORK IS 'EAVEN! -BUT BECAUSE 'E WUZ POOR -AN' COULDN'T SPEAK T' ANYONE - 'E MISSED ALL TH' FUN....
12-20
Reg. U. S. Pat. Off.; Copyright, 1939, by News Syndicate Co., Inc.
...'E WANTS T' GO BACK THERE WITH 'IS MONEY AN' NEW EDUCATION AN' BE EMPEROR O' TH' CITY!
EMPEROR? ...YOU'RE JOSHIN' US, BLAZE!
CROSS ME 'EART! THIS SINGH-SINGH IS INGENIOUS, LIKE YE SAY — BUT 'E'S THICK-'EADED IN MOST THINGS! 'E THINKS ALL 'E'LL 'AVE T' DO T' BE EMPEROR O' NEW YORK IS T' PULL A GHENGIS KHAN...
... MOVE IN, KICK OUT TH' WEAK OPPOSITION, BUY OUT TH' STRONG! GET CONTROL O' TH' DRINKIN' AN' GAMBLIN', AN SCARE TH' BRITCHES OFF TH' PEACEFUL CITIZENS... PRESTO! YER BOSS!
HMMM! THAT'S NOT SO STUPID! WITH THE EXCEPTION OF A FEW DETAILS, THAT SYSTEM HAS WORKED FOR YEARS!
MILTON CANIFF

SO MUCH FOR THIS SINGH-SINGH'S AMBITION! OUR JOB IS TO BE CERTAIN THAT HE DOESN'T TAKE A FANCY TO APRIL WHEN HE ARRIVES!
WE'RE LUCKY! ONLY WE THREE AN' ME DAUGHTER KNOW YOU TWO AIN'T REALLY HITCHED! 'E'LL 'AVE NO EYE FER A WEDDED WOMAN!
12-21
I DECLARE IT CREEPS ME, JUS' THINKIN' OF IT! CAN'T WE GO AWAY?
THE INVADER LINES ARE IN ONE DIRECTION, WASTE LAND IN ANOTHER — AN' FLOOD STAGE RIVERS ON TH REMAININ' SIDES! 'TWOULDN'T BE SAFE!
SHUSH!
Reg. U. S. Pat. Off.; Copyright, 1939, by News Syndicate Co., Inc.
...HI'D 'AVE SWORE SOMEONE COUGHED OUT 'ERE! MUST BE ME NERVES TWITCHIN'!
MILTON CANIFF

NO ONE ELSE DOWN YET?
IS NO! BLING BLEAKFAST, CHOP, CHOP!
12-22
Reg. U. S. Pat. Off.; Copyright, 1939, by News Syndicate Co., Inc.
HEY! WHAT'S THIS AT MY PLATE?
...A LITTLE CHINESE GODDESS OF LOVE! THAT'S ODD...
MILTON CANIFF

MORNIN', MISTER RYAN!
WHY-AH- GOOD MORNING, APRIL! SLEEP WELL?
12-23
WELL AS I COULD - STEWIN' 'BOUT THIS SINGH-SINGH MAN... WHAT'S THAT?
OH, THAT... IT'S A CHINESE CHARM... IT'S A GIFT!
FOR ME? - OH, MISTER RYAN, HOW DOWNRIGHT THOUGHTFUL! IT'S BEAUTIFUL!!
Reg. U. S. Pat. Off.; Copyright, 1939, by News Syndicate Co., Inc.
WELL- I...
NOW DON'T YOU SAY IT'S JUST A LI'L THING! I'VE BEEN FRANTIC FOR ONE SINCE I SAW THE COLLECTION MISS CHEERY BLAZE HAS IN HER ROOM!!
MILTON CANIFF

TERRY AND THE PIRATES
by MILTON CANIFF
Reg. U. S. Pat. Off.; Copyright, 1939, by News Syndicate Co., Inc.
WHO'S THERE?
YOU JITTERY TOO, CAP'N BLAZE?
BUCKO! WITH THAT RASCAL, SINGH-SINGH, DUE 'ERE ANY DAY HI'VE BEEN LOSIN' A MESS O' DREAM TIME!
WHERE'S TH' WEE APRIL LASSIE ?
SHE WENT TO SLEEP HOURS AGO! I'VE BEEN TRAMPING THE FLOOR TRYING TO THINK OF SOME WAY TO CROSS UP THIS COLORFUL COSSACK WHEN HE ARRIVES!
WE MIGHT SHIP YE OUT TILL 'E'S GONE... BUT ME DAUGHTER, OR ONE O' TH' MEN, IS SURE T' TELL TH'-BLIGHTER YOU WUZ 'ERE! 'E'D BE FIT T' TIE HIF 'E 'EARD THERE WUZ A COMELY WENCH 'ERE AN' 'E'D MISSED SEEIN' 'ER!
YEAH! I'VE THOUGHT OF ALL THAT!
SUN'S RISING! AT LEAST THE COUNTRY LOOKS PEACEFUL!
WOT'S THAT ?
SOUNDS LIKE MACHINE GUN FIRE... !!
ALARM!
TAKE THIS, RYAN! WE'LL NEED EVERY MAN! FOLLOW ME!
RIGHT!
SHOOTIN'S IN TH' COURTYARD! MUST BE AN ATTACK FROM TH' BACK GATE! RUSH 'EM BEFORE THEY REACH TH' MAIN BUILDINGS!
DON'T LOOK SO DOWNRIGHT MENACIN'! IT'S JUS' APRIL WISHIN' Y'ALL A GOOD OL' DIXIE STYLE MERRY CHRISTMAS!!
12-24

WHAT STRANGE EMOTION AGITATES YOU, MY FRIEND?
BY THE BEARDS OF MY ANCESTORS, THESE WESTERN PEOPLE PRODUCE MIRACLES!
12-25
WHAT WIZARDRY IS THIS?
YOU WOULD NOT BELIEVE THE STORY! COME, I WILL REVEAL IT TO YOUR OWN EYES!
MILTON CANIFF
WITNESS! WHERE YESTERDAY THERE WAS AN EMPTY HALL— TODAY A LIVING TREE GROWS FROM THE FLOOR, BEARING FRUIT OF LIGHTED TAPERS! ONE CAN BUT MARVEL!
Reg. U. S. Pat. Off.: Copyright, 1939, by News Syndicate Co., Inc.

...YOU CAN SEE YOU HAVEN'T A CHANCE! DROP THAT GUN!...
?
12-26
...YOU'VE MADE YOUR LAST CLEVER MOVE! NOW IT IS OUR TURN...
THAT ISN'T BLAZE'S VOICE! THE OLD BOY'S IN TROUBLE!
...WILL OUR FRIENDS ESCAPE THIS TIME? LISTEN TOMORROW EVENING FOR ANOTHER ELECTRICALLY TRANSCRIBED BROADCAST OF..
WOT AILS YE, BUCKO? DON'T YE LIKE THE ARRANGEMENT O' FURNITURE?
MILTON CANIFF
Reg. U. S. Pat. Off.: Copyright, 1939, by News Syndicate Co., Inc.

I DIDN'T KNOW YOU HAD THIS RADIO SET, BLAZE!
RIGHT'O! HIT'S ME PET! TWO WAY SYSTEM, WITH SHORT WAVE POWERFUL ENOUGH T' GET TH' UNITED STATES! RIGHT SMART, WOT?
12-27
HIT'S ME ONLY CONTACT WITH WOT'S GOIN' ON IN TH' WORLD! HI OFTEN LIS--- 'EY! WOT'S THIS!
HIT WUZ THE INVADER ARMY STATION... WARNIN' OUTPOSTS THAT SINGH-SINGH IS ON 'IS WAY INTO CHINA WITH A LOAD O' GUNS... WHICH MEANS 'E'LL BE 'ERE IN NO TIME!! COMFORTIN' THOUGHT, AIN'T IT?
MILTON CANIFF
Reg. U. S. Pat. Off.: Copyright, 1939, by News Syndicate Co., Inc.

NO USE SITTING HERE STEWING ABOUT IT! WHEN SINGH-SINGH COMES, HE'LL COME! I'M TURNING IN, BLAZE!
RIGHT'O, PATRICK, ME LAD!
12-28
ME POOR 'EADS FIT T' BUST WITH TH' DEVILISH LUCK WOT PURSUES ME! ZOOKS AN' ZOUNDS!
MASTER! MASTER!
THE SENTINEL WHO AWAITED THE BOAT BEARING THE GOLD TO PAY SINGH-SINGH HAS RETURNED FROM THE RIVER!
MILTON CANIFF
ALAS, MASTER, THE STREAM RACES AT FLOOD STAGE... THE GOLD BOAT ATTEMPTED TO CROSS— AND CAPSIZED IN MID-RIVER!
OOOOOHHHH!
Reg. U. S. Pat. Off.: Copyright, 1939, by News Syndicate Co., Inc.

HAHAHA! NO GIRL FOR SINGH-SINGH... AND NOW NO MONEY TO BUY HIS GUNS!
12-29
Reg. U. S. Pat. Off.: Copyright, 1939, by News Syndicate Co., Inc.
'OW DID YE KNOW ALL THIS, WENCH?
I MAKE IT MY BUSINESS TO LEARN ANYTHING THAT MAY BE DISCONCERTING TO YOU! I HAVE MY METHODS!
BLIGH'ME, LASS, HI'VE TRIED BEIN' A PROPER PARENT TO YE! WHY MUST YE PLAGUE TH' WITS OUT O' ME WHEN HI'M BURDENED T' TH' SCUPPERS WITH SORE TRIALS?
MILTON CANIFF
OH, I CAN BE HELPFUL WHEN I CHOOSE... SINGH-SINGH WOULD GLADLY GIVE YOU CREDIT — IF YOU OFFERED HIM SUCH A PRIZE AS THE AMERICAN GIRL! AND THAT'S EXACTLY WHAT YOU'VE BEEN TURNING OVER IN YOUR MIND....

WOT SORT O SHE-DEVIL BE YE, WANTIN' ME T' SHIP THIS AMERICAN LASS OFF WITH THAT BLOKE SINGH-SINGH?
I AM LIKE YOU IN GOING DIRECTLY AFTER SOMETHING I WANT!
12-30
YE MEAN YE LONGS FER PATRICK RYAN? BLOW ME TOP, GAL, 'E'D 'AVE NO EYES FER TH' LIKES O' YE! 'E'S BEEN FANCIED BY TH' PRETTIEST!
I HAVE NO ILLUSIONS ABOUT MY CHARMS...
Reg. U. S. Pat. Off.: Copyright, 1939, by News Syndicate Co., Inc.
... BUT IF YOU SENT THE GIRL WITH SINGH-SINGH, YOU WOULD HAVE TO HOLD RYAN HERE SO HE WOULDN'T GO AFTER HER....
... GIVEN ENOUGH TIME — AND SUFFICIENT LONELINESS, MR. RYAN WOULD BEGIN TO SEE ME IN A DIFFERENT LIGHT... IF I AM WRONG — THEN SO ARE HALF THE BOOKS THAT HAVE EVER BEEN WRITTEN!
MILTON CANIFF

TERRY
AND THE PIRATES
by MILTON CANIFF
Reg. U. S. Pat. Off.: Copyright, 1939, by News Syndicate Co., Inc.
BEHOLD! THE LINES OF CONCERN DEEPEN ON THE FAT FACE! THE SEASONED SCHEMER IS IN A DILEMMA TOO GREAT FOR HIS FEEBLE MENTAL POWERS!
AN INTERCEPTED INVADER WIRELESS WARNING HAS TOLD YOU OF THE APPROACH OF THE GUN-RUNNER, SINGH-SINGH! NOW YOU MUST BE READY WITH CASH TO PAY FOR HIS WARES — AS WELL AS THE ENGLISH-SPEAKING WIFE FOR HIS HAREM!
... AND YOU KNOW THAT, IN THE ABSENCE OF THE MONEY, YOU COULD MOLLIFY HIM BY PRODUCING SUCH A RICH PRIZE AS THE AMERICAN GIRL! BUT YOU HAVE TOLD THE HANDSOME RYAN MAN YOU WERE HIS TRUE FRIEND — AND WOULD NOT THINK OF SUCH A THING! WRITHE, MY DESPISED PARENT!
GIT OUT O' ME SIGHT, WENCH, BEFORE I FERGIT YER ME OWN DAUGHTER AN' TONGUE-LASH YE IN A WAY NOT PROPER FER A LOVIN' FATHER! AVAST!
I GO, WILLINGLY! YOU ARE NO FEAST FOR MY EYES!
WOT 'AVE HI DONE, ASIDE FROM ME MANY CRIMES, T' DESERVE SUCH A TYPHOON O' TROUBLES? THAT SWAB, SINGH-SINGH, AN' 'IS TOUGH BLOKES'LL BE AROUND ME EARS IN A TWINKLE — AN' TH' FUR IS SURE T' FLY!

MASTER, MASTER! A GRAVE CONSPIRACY...
WOT? MORE GRIEF? BUST LOOSE WITH HIT, CUE-BALL!
SINCE THE AMERICAN, RYAN, DISCOVERED THE PRESENCE OF OUR ALL-POWERFUL SHORT-WAVE WIRELESS, I HAVE NOTED HIS INTEREST IN SAME!
WOT'S CONSPIRIN' ABOUT SUCH DOIN'S, YE DROOP?
...EVEN NOW HE SITS WITH AMERICAN WOMAN-CHILD BEFORE THE SPEAKING MECHANISM! THEY LISTEN TO STRANGE CODE WHICH THEY INTERPRET WITH DESIGNS ON FLOOR!
BLOW ME TOP! CAN HIT BE THAT ME PAL RYAN IS PLOTTIN' T' DO ME DIRT?
THEY ARE SO ABSORBED WITH THEIR STRANGE MESSAGES, IT IS POSSIBLE TO OBSERVE WITHOUT DETECTION! BEHOLD...
12-31
OUT OF THE HUDDLE NOW... DOUBLE WING BACK TO THE RIGHT SAFETY DEEP FOR A QUICK BOOT... IT'S SNAPPED... IT'S A REVERSE... NUMBER 43 HAS IT... LATERALS TO NUMBER 16... HE'S CLEAR... TO THE 30-20-10... HE'S OVER!! IT'S 13 TO 7 AND THE CROWD IS WILD!!

CARE TO GO FOR A WALK IN THE RAIN, KITTEN?
WHY, THAT WOULD JUS' PLEASE ME T' PIECES, MR. RYAN!
1-1
YOU NO GO!
OKAY! LET'S STROLL OVER TO THE PATH UP THE HILL, APRIL!
FORBIDDEN!
Reg. U. S. Pat. Off.: Copyright, 1940, by News Syndicate Co., Inc.
MERCY! I RECKON WE JUS' HAVE T' STAY INSIDE TH' WIRE FENCE!
THAT'S WHY I WANTED TO TAKE THIS WALK... TO FIND THAT OUT! BLAZE ADVISED US TO STAY HERE UNTIL THIS SINGH-SINGH GUY ARRIVES! IN REALITY, WE MUST! BABY, WE'VE BEEN SOLD OUT!
MILTON CANIFF

OH, MR. RYAN, I'M SHAKIN'! I THOUGHT YOU FELT WE COULD TRUST CAP'N BLAZE! BUT WE KNOW NOW THAT WE'RE PRISONERS!
THE OLD BOY'S ON THE SPOT... IF HE COULD DELIVER YOU TO SINGH-SINGH IT WOULD BE A FANCY BARGAIN!
1-2
OH, THAT'S TOO HORRIBLE T' EVEN THINK ABOUT! YOU WON'T LET THAT HAPPEN... TELL ME YOU WON'T!
BRAVE WORDS WON'T HELP NOW, KITTEN... WE'VE GOT TO USE OUR HEADS! HOW'S THE OLD BRAIN CLICKING?
MERCY, I'M IN SUCH A FIDGET I CAN'T THINK OF MY OWN NAME T'SAVE ME!
THAT'S FINE...
Reg. U. S. Pat. Off.: Copyright, 1940, by News Syndicate Co., Inc.
WHY, WHATEVER DO YOU MEAN?
JUST WHAT I SAID, SUGAH.... THE PLAN I HAVE CALLS FOR COMPLETE MENTAL COLLAPSE! LISTEN....
MILTON CANIFF

TWIDDLE-WIT DUG UP THIS OLD PAIR OF SPECTACLES! I TOLD HIM YOU NEEDED THEM TO READ WITH!
OH, MERCY, I HOPE THIS WORKS OUT!
1-3
IT WILL, IF YOU PLAY YOUR PART! REMEMBER WHAT I TOLD YOU—WE'LL BEAT THIS THING YET! I'M GOING TO SET THE STAGE! CHIN UP, KITTEN!
YOU..?
MIND IF I COME IN, MISS BLAZE?
Reg. U. S. Pat. Off.; Copyright, 1940, by News Syndicate Co., Inc.
I WANTED TO CHECK UP ON THE AUTHENTICITY OF A CHINESE LOVE CHARM I HAVE, AND I KNEW YOU'D BE THE ONLY PERSON HERE WHO COULD POSSIBLY KNOW ANYTHING ABOUT SUCH A SCHOLARLY SUBJECT!
???
MILTON CANIFF

THIS IS AN AMAZING LIBRARY FOR SUCH A REMOTE PLACE! YOU MUST RECEIVE MUCH PLEASURE FROM YOUR BOOKS!
WHY-AH-YES...I DO!
1-4
I HAVE ALWAYS ADMIRED WOMEN WITH REAL BRAINS... A RARE QUALITY! ...ABOUT THIS LOVE CHARM... IT'S AN EXQUISITE PIECE... I WISH I KNEW WHO WAS SO GENEROUS AS TO LEAVE IT AT MY PLATE!
PERHAPS IT WAS YOUR—AH-WIFE!
NOT APRIL! SHE WOULDN'T KNOW A LOVE CHARM FROM A CIGAR LIGHTER! POOR SILLY KID... GETTING A KICK OUT OF YOUR FATHER'S MEN THINKING WE WERE MARRIED... I WISH SHE COULD TALK ABOUT OTHER THINGS BESIDES MEN, AND DANCING, AND CLOTHES!
MILTON CANIFF
Reg. U. S. Pat. Off.; Copyright, 1940, by News Syndicate Co., Inc.
.... AH! A SET OF SHAKESPEARE! "THE MERCHANT OF VENICE" HAS THE PORTIA PART UNDERSCORED! THAT'S JUST THE ROLE YOU COULD PLAY TO PERFECTION—AND I'LL WAGER YOU'VE MEMORIZED IT—HAVEN'T YOU?
YES...

SO YOU'VE LEARNED THE PART OF PORTIA IN "THE MERCHANT OF VENICE"!.... HOW I WOULD ENJOY HEARING YOU DO SOME PASSAGES FROM THE PLAY!
YOU-YOU WOULD? REALLY?
1-5
BY ALL MEANS! IT HAS BEEN SO LONG SINCE I HAVE BEEN NEAR ANYONE—ESPECIALLY A WOMAN—WHO APPRECIATED SUCH THINGS!
I WOULD BE DELIGHTED TO READ FOR YOU—IF YOU REALLY WISH ME TO!
BUT OF COURSE I DO! THIS IS NOT THE TIME NOR PLACE, HOWEVER! I MUST GO NOW—BUT SOON, WHEN THE STAGE IS SET—AND THE MOMENT IS JUST RIGHT! GOODBYE—FOR NOW!
MILTON CANIFF
Reg. U. S. Pat. Off.; Copyright, 1940, by News Syndicate Co., Inc.

SO MISS BLAZE RECITES SHAKESPEARE!... THAT MAY BE THE DIFFERENCE BETWEEN A FADEOUT AND A PULL-OUT FOR APRIL AND ME!
AT THIS MOMENT—NEAR THE OUTER GATE
HE COMES! HE COMES!
MILTON CANIFF
Reg. U. S. Pat. Off.; Copyright, 1940, by News Syndicate Co., Inc.

TERRY AND THE PIRATES
by MILTON CANIFF
WHAT'S THAT RACKET ?
WOW! IT'S LIKE THE GRAND OPENING SPECTACLE OF EVERY CIRCUS I EVER SAW!
SINGH-SINGH!
SINGH-SINGH!
THIS GUY MUST BE THE SORT WHO HAS HIMSELF PAGED IN HOTEL LOBBIES!
SINGH-SINGH!
WHAT A BUILDUP! THIS SINGH-SINGH HAD BETTER BE GOOD, OR I'LL ASK FOR MY MONEY BACK!

SINGH-SINGH!
1-8
STUP!
HALLUH, KEPTIN BLAZER! YUH VANTA WRASSLE?
Reg. U.S. Pat. Off.; Copyright, 1940, by News Syndicate Co., Inc.
MILTON CANIFF

1-9
YOU DUN'T WRASSLE SO GUDE, KEPTIN BLAZER!
BLAWST YER 'IDE, SINGH-SINGH, YOU AIN'T GOT TH' MANNERS OF A MOUNTAIN GOAT... THOUGH THERE'S OTHER SIMILARITIES!
Reg. U.S. Pat. Off.; Copyright, 1940, by News Syndicate Co., Inc.
SINK-SINK DUN'T NEED MANNERS! YOU SOFT! SINK-SINK PLANTY TOFF! NOW TALK BIZNESS!
SINK-SINK BRING PLANTY GONS! YOU GOT VOT SINK-SINK VANTS?
YEE-E-S, HI'VE GOT HIT!
MILTON CANIFF

HOSTLE, KEPTIN BLAZER! YOU BRING VOT SINK-SINK VANTS! DOBBLE QUEEK!!
WON'T BE LONG—HI'M SENDIN' A BOY!
1-10
BETTER BE PLANTY GUDE!
BEST HI COULD GET, SINGH-SINGH! YOU KNOW ME!
IS HERE!
COME IN AN' 'AVE A LOOK!
Reg. U.S. Pat. Off.; Copyright, 1940, by News Syndicate Co., Inc.
AHHHH! PAPPERMEENT!!
MILTON CANIFF

AHHH!
1-11
OOOH! WALKEENK STEECK!
HMMM!
Reg. U.S. Pat. Off.; Copyright, 1940, by News Syndicate Co., Inc.
NUT BAD! NOW BRING ON VELCOME BANQUET FOR SINK-SINK! WAN BIG PEEG!
WAS THAT AN ORDER—OR A BIT O' SELF CRITICISM?
MILTON CANIFF

YER WELCOME BANQUET'S COMIN' UP, SINGH-SINGH! TH' LADS'LL SERVE HIT IN 'ERE!
LADS? NO GUDE! GOT NO CLASS!
1-12
Reg. U. S. Pat. Off.: Copyright, 1940, by News Syndicate Co., Inc.
SINK-SINK SERVED ONLY BY VIMMINS! CALL IN HAREM!
'OW NOW, SINGH-SINGH! HI DIDN'T KNOW YE ALLOWED YER WIVES T' EAT WITH YE!
NO EAT—TASTE! IF WIFE GO TO SLEEP SINK-SINK KNOCK KEPTIN BLAZER TO SLEEP! SIMPLE, NO?
MILTON CANIFF

NUT BAD PEEG! ALMOST GUDE ENOFF TO BE VORTHY OF SINK-SINK!
NO PIG COULD BE THAT GOOD!
1-13
HAND ME STEECK OF PAPPERMEENT WHILE WAIT FOR NEXT COURSE!
BLIGH'ME... HI KIN SEE WHY YE NEEDS THAT LEATHER BELT!
Reg. U. S. Pat. Off.: Copyright, 1940, by News Syndicate Co., Inc.
VOT'S DELAY? WHO DARES HOLD OP SINK-SINK'S EATINK?
MILTON CANIFF

TERRY AND THE PIRATES by MILTON CANIFF
EAT 'EARTY, SINGH-SINGH! THAT THERE'S TH' BEST PIG IN TH' PLACE... AN' TH' BEST PEPPERMINT CANDY I COULD GET FROM TH' COAST BEFORE TH' FLOODS!
VY NUT? SINK-SINK ALVAYS GET BEST! VOT DELAYS LAST COURSE?
I DUNNO! YE INSISTED ON BEIN' SERVED BY YER WIVES SO I COULDN'T POISON YE! MEBBE THEY'VE STRUCK!
HO! THEY'RE STANDIN' 'ERE STARIN' AT RYAN! —EVEN AS MANY A LASSIE BEFORE 'EM!
WHO DARE DELAY SINK-SINK'S EATINK? BRING HIM IN!
NOW DON'T GET HUFFY, SINGH-SINGH! THIS 'ERE'S ME GUEST, PATRICK RYAN!
IRISHER! SINK-SINK DUN'T LIKE IRISHERS! YOU VANTA WRASSLE?
NO, I CAN'T SAY THAT I DO!
'EY, SINGH-SINGH—WHERE'S YER MANNERS?
SINK-SINK DUN'T NEED MANNERS! DUN'T LIKE YOUR FACE! YOU WRASSLE!

I'M NOT SO CRAZY ABOUT YOUR FACE — BUT I STILL DON'T CARE TO WRESTLE!
SINK-SINK MOSS YOU OP!
LIKE DIS!
... STRANGE DUCK, ISN'T HE? SMELLS OF PEPPERMINT!

DID YOU NOT HEAR OF THE MOST AMAZING OCCURRENCE? THE BRUTAL SINGH-SINGH FORCED THE YOUNG AMERICAN TO WRESTLE —!
IN PAYMENT FOR HIS BAD MANNERS, THE WALRUS-FACED ONE LIES WITHOUT SENSE UPON THE FLOOR!
1-15
Reg. U. S. Pat. Off.: Copyright, 1940, by News Syndicate Co., Inc.
TH' FAT'S IN TH' GALLEY NOW, PATRICK! YE'VE FLUNG SINGH-SINGH ... AN' 'E'LL 'AVE 'IS BUTCHERS AT OUR THROATS FER REVENGE! — IF 'IS NECK AIN'T BUSTED — HI 'OPE!
COULDN'T BREAK HIS NECK — HE HASN'T ANY! CALL FOR SOME WATER ... WE MAY BE ABLE TO SMOOTH IT OVER!
WHAT HAPPENED, KILLER? WE WERE WRESTLING — AND YOU PASSED OUT! MUST HAVE BEEN THAT BIG MEAL YOU JUST ATE!
HUH? — OH, YUP! DAT'S SO! TOC MUCH KENDY!
MILTON CANIFF

YOU WRASSLE PUTTY GUDE FOR IRISHER! SINK-SINK DUN'T LIKE IRISHERS MOST TIME! VE FINISH WRASSLE VEN SINK-SINK AIN'T EAT SO MUCH KENDY!
OKAY, PAL, ANY TIME! ... YOU CAN TEACH ME SOME TRICKS!
1-16
Reg. U. S. Pat. Off.: Copyright, 1940, by News Syndicate Co., Inc.
VELL, KEPTIN BLAZER ... VE GET DOWN TO BIZNIZ, YUP?
WELL, HI TELL YE, SINGH-SINGH ... HIT'S THIS WAY ..
THE CAP'N MEANS YOU SHOULD HAVE SOME RELAXATION AFTER YOUR LONG STAY IN THE HILLS! ... SOME ENTERTAINMENT!
SHOO! VOT YOU GOT, DENCING GELS?
NO, INDEED! ... CAP'N BLAZE TELLS ME YOU'RE LEARNING CORRECT ENGLISH — SO WE HAVE SOME HIGH CLASS THEATRICALS FOR YOU!
MILTON CANIFF

I KNOW A STUDIOUS FELLOW LIKE YOU WOULD PREFER DRAMA TO DANCING GIRLS! I'LL GET THINGS STARTED!
SMART IRISHER! HE KNOW HIGH CLASS GENT WHEN SEE ME!
1-17
Reg. U. S. Pat. Off.; Copyright, 1940, by News Syndicate Co., Inc.
VILE DAT IRISHER FIX BEEG SHOW YOU AN' SINK-SINK TALK BIZNIZ, HUH, BLAZER?
WELL, HI... AH...
VOT'S D' HESITATE, KEPTIN BLAZER? ...YOU MEBBE DUN'T GOT D' MONEY FOR D' GONS — AN' D' NEW VIFE FOR SINK-SINK?
AW, NAW, HIT AIN'T THAT, SINGHY — HIT'S JUST THAT HI 'AD A LITTLE SURPRISE HI WANTED YE T' 'AVE BEFORE 'AND! LOOK!
CHUCKLUTS! VITH NOTS! KEPTIN BLAZER, SOMETIMES SINK-SINK T'INKS YOU NOT HALF SO DIRTY CROOK AS I KNOW YOU ARE!
MILTON CANIFF

APRIL, WE CAN'T HOLD OFF THE CLIMAX OF THIS PARTY VERY LONG! YOU READY?
I RECKON SO, MISTER RYAN... BUT I'M SO SKITTERY I'M NIGH T' SWOONIN'!
1-18
I'M GOING FOR CHEERY BLAZE NOW! ON YOUR TOES!
I'VE BEEN ON 'EM SO LONG, MY LEGS ARE SLEEPIN'!
Reg. U. S. Pat. Off.; Copyright, 1940, by News Syndicate Co., Inc.
MISS CHEERY... IT'S PATRICK RYAN! MAY I COME IN?
INDEED!
" BY MY TROTH, NERISSA, MY LITTLE BODY IS AWEARY OF THIS GREAT WORLD... "
MILTON CANIFF

MARVELOUS, MISS BLAZE! WHAT A PLEASURE IT IS TO HEAR SHAKESPEARE DONE SO BEAUTIFULLY!
NO ONE HAS EVER GIVEN ME A COMPLIMENT BEFORE!
1-19
YOUR FATHER DOESN'T KNOW WHAT TALENT YOU HAVE! I WANT YOU TO COME DOWNSTAIRS AND GIVE A RECITAL WHILE SINGH-SINGH IS HERE! I TOLD HIM I HAD THE SURPRISE OF HIS LIFE WAITING!
SINGH-SINGH!
YES! HE SAYS THERE IS NO CULTURE OUT HERE — I BOASTED THAT THERE IS — NOW I MUST PROVE MY POINT — OR LOSE FACE!
I WILL GO DOWN AND RECITE... BUT NOT FOR SINGH-SINGH! IT WILL BE FOR TWO REASONS — TO PROVE YOU ARE RIGHT ... AND TO SHOW UP THE STUPID PRETTINESS OF THE GIRL WHO POSES AS YOUR WIFE! COME!
MILTON CANIFF
Reg. U. S. Pat. Off.; Copyright, 1940, by News Syndicate Co., Inc.

THANK TH' STARS, YE'VE ARRIVED, RYAN! HI CAN'T STALL THE OLD BLOKE MUCH LONGER! WOT'S UP TH' WIND?
WAIT, YOU'LL SEE! SINGH-SINGH, WE'RE GOING TO DO SOME SCENES FROM " THE MERCHANT OF VENICE"! HIGH CLASS STUFF!
1-20
MERCHUNT UV VENUZ — YOU MEAN HIGH CLESS HOT DUG SELLER?
NO, THIS IS SHAKESPEARE — FINEST ENGLISH EVER WRITTEN!
I'LL GIVE YOU YOUR CUE... ALL SET?
OF COURSE!
Reg. U. S. Pat. Off.; Copyright, 1940, by News Syndicate Co., Inc.
MILTON CANIFF
"...AND HERE, I TAKE IT, IS THE DOCTOR COME... GIVE ME YOUR HAND. COME YOU FROM OLD BELLARIO?"
"I DID, MY LORD"
HA! ACTUHS! A SHOW... FREE FOR NUTTIN! IS GUDE!

TERRY AND THE PIRATES
by MILTON CANIFF
Reg. U. S. Pat. Off.: Copyright, 1940, by News Syndicate Co., Inc.
INSTEAD OF BEING ANGRY WITH PAT FOR THROWING HIM, SINGH-SINGH TAKES A LIKING TO THE "IRISHER"...
TO STALL OFF BLAZE'S HAVING TO TALK BUSINESS WITH THE GUN-RUNNER, PAT PROMISES A FREE SHOW WHICH WILL IMPROVE SINGH-SINGH'S ENGLISH .... HE HAS LEARNED THAT CHEERY BLAZE ASPIRES TO BE AN ACTRESS .... SO...
BLOW ME TOPPER: RYAN'S GOT ME DAUGHTER OUT THERE SPOUTIN' SHAKESPEARE! WOT'S 'IS SCHEME? HI DON'T CATCH ON!
THE QUALITY OF MERCY IS NOT STRAINED, IT DROPPETH AS THE GENTLE RAIN FROM HEAVEN ..."
"... UPON THE PLACE BENEATH: IT IS TWICE BLEST; IT BLESSETH HIM THAT GIVES, AND HIM THAT TAKES ...."
HEY, DAT'S GUDE!
BLAWST ME, SINGH-SINGH'S LAPPIN' HIT UP! — BUT HI'M IN TH' DARK — WOT'S THAT FOXY RYAN UP TO?
THROUGH THE COURTROOM SCENE OF "THE MERCHANT OF VENICE" PAT READS THE OTHER LINES WHILE CHEERY BLAZE ACTS THE PART OF PORTIA, THE WOMAN LAWYER
"... WELL, PEACE BE WITH YOU."
THAT'S THE END OF THE ACT, GENTLEMEN! HOW DID YOU LIKE IT?
IS GUDE! PLANTY GUDE!
DON'T YOU THINK THAT'S BEAUTIFUL ENGLISH, SINGH-SINGH?
SHOO! SINK-SINK DUN'T KNOW VOT IS ALL ABOUT — BUT SHOO LISTENS GUDE!
RYAN'S GOT THE OL' GOAT IN A GOOD HUMOR — BUT WHAT HAPPENS NOW?
THAT'S ONLY A SMALL PART OF SHAKESPEARE'S WORK, SINGH-SINGH! THE YOUNG LADY KNOWS MUCH MORE!
HA! SINK-SINK KETCH ON! DAT GEL IS NEW VIFE FOR HAREM! SHE BEST ENGLISH SPEECHER SO FAR! BIG SOOPRISE!
WHAT?
I SEE IT ALL NOW! THIS MAN RYAN FLATTERED ME INTO RECITING — SO SINGH-SINGH WOULD WANT ME FOR HIS HAREM! — THUS SAVING THAT BEAUTIFUL LITTLE FOOL WHO TRAILS AFTER HIM !!!
BOOTIFUL LIDDLE FOOL? VOT'S DIS? SOMEBUDDY HOLD OUT ON SINK-SINK?
THERE'S A PRETTY AMERICAN GIRL UPSTAIRS WHO POSES AS THIS MAN'S WIFE — SO YOU WON'T TAKE HER FOR YOUR HAREM! BUT SHE ISN'T MARRIED TO HIM!
SO! DAT IRISHER PLAY TRICKS! BRING PURTY GEL DOWN BEFORE SINK-SINK TEAR OP JOINT!
OOOOH!
YOU LYING DOG! I MIGHT HAVE KNOWN YOU'D DO ANYTHING TO SAVE THAT DOLL-FACED CHILD! — BUT IT DIDN'T WORK!
SHOT OP, VOMAN! SINK-SINK TAKE CARE OF IRISHER LATER! NOW TAKE LOOK AT DIS DAME!
MASTER SINGH-SINGH WANT BEAUTIFUL AMERICAN GIRL! YOU SHOW WHERE IS SHE!
OOOHH! WILL DO! MISSY! PLEASE TO COME OUT!
1-21
BOO!!

AT THE END OF CHEERY'S PERFORMANCE AS PORTIA, SINGH-SINGH THINKS THE SHOW WAS ARRANGED TO INTRODUCE HIM TO THE ENGLISH-SPEAKING GIRL WHO IS TO BE THE NEW WIFE FOR HIS HAREM!!
OH, NO! THIS MAN RYAN FLATTERED ME INTO SHOWING OFF—TO PROTECT THE PRETTY FOOL UPSTAIRS!
SINK-SINK HEARD, ALL DAT, VOMAN! YOU SHOT OP!
1-22
DIS IRISHER HAS PURTY GEL WHO ACT AS HIS VIFE—SO SINK-SINK DUN'T TAKE HER AVAY! I FIX HIM LATER! NOW SINK-SINK'S MEN GO OPSTAIRS TO GET DIS DAME!
Reg. U. S. Pat. Off.: Copyright, 1940, by News Syndicate Co., Inc.
COMES ONLY WOMAN WE FIND IN HOUSE!
BOO! I'M A CHIMPANZEE!
MILTON CANIFF

OOOHH! HANDLE-BARS!
VOT'S DIS?
THAT'S THE GIRL I WAS TRYING TO SAVE FROM YOU!
1-23
TICKLE!
HELP, IRISHER! FORGET ABOUT SAFE HER FROM ME! SAFE ME FROM HER!!
MILTON CANIFF
Reg. U. S. Pat. Off.: Copyright, 1940, by News Syndicate Co., Inc.

HERE, HERE, YOU CAN'T TREAT SINGH-SINGH LIKE THAT! HE WANTS YOU FOR HIS HAREM!
GOODY! GOODY! GOODY!
1-24
Reg. U. S. Pat. Off.: Copyright, 1940, by News Syndicate Co., Inc.
HAREM! HAREM! HAREM!
SINK-SINK GO!
BUT SHE'S NOT REALLY MARRIED... AND SHE SPEAKS ENGLISH....
SINK-SINK DUN'T CARE IF SHE INWENTED ENGLISH! GUDE-BYE!
MILTON CANIFF

'E'S GONE!
... HE'S GATHERING UP HIS MEN AND LEAVING THE COURTYARD!
1-25
Reg. U. S. Pat. Off.: Copyright, 1940, by News Syndicate Co., Inc.
OH, MISTER RYAN, I FEEL SUCH A FOOL!
YOU WERE SUPERB, KITTEN! YOU SAVED THE DAY!
SAVED THE DAY, INDEED! YOU OPTIMISTIC FOOLS! YOU HAVE HURT SINGH-SINGH'S DIGNITY—AND HE'LL HAVE REVENGE WHEN HE CALMS DOWN!
BLIGH'ME, RYAN, ME DAUGHTER'S RIGHT! TH' NAWSTY BLOKE'LL BE ABOUT OUR EARS!
... NOT ONLY THAT... TO FURTHER YOUR OWN PURPOSES YOU HAVE MADE A FOOL OF ME! IF SINGH-SINGH DOESN'T CRUSH YOU, I SHALL!
MILTON CANIFF

CAN I TAKE THIS STUFF OFF MY TEETH AN' GET FIXED UP, MISTER RYAN?
YES, KITTEN, I DON'T THINK YOU'LL NEED TO GO INTO YOUR ACT AGAIN!
1-26
Reg. U. S. Pat. Off.; Copyright, 1940, by News Syndicate Co., Inc.
WELL, BLAZE, OUR CARDS ARE DOWN NOW! YOU HAD US HELD HERE TO USE APRIL AS A FINAL SALVE TO SINGH-SINGH — IN CASE HE GOT TOUGH ABOUT NO PAYMENT FOR HIS GUNS!
YER ACCUSIN' ME 'ARSH, PATRICK!
YOU'D SELL OUT YOUR BEST FRIEND, YOU OLD ROGUE!.... BUT NOW SINGH-SINGH WILL DEMAND HIS MONEY — YOU WON'T BE ABLE TO EITHER PAY — OR PRODUCE A NEW WIFE FOR HIM...
SINCE WE'RE ALL IN THE SAME STEW, WE MIGHT AS WELL COOPERATE! — WE MAY BE ABLE TO OUTSMART THE OLD WALRUS-FACE!
SINGH-SINGH SETTIN' OUT ON THEM 'ILLS WITH FIVE TIMES AS MANY GUNS AN' MEN AS US — AN' 'IM GETTIN' MADDER EACH MINUTE... HI'M GLAD HI AIN'T A PESSIMIST!
MILTON CANIFF

SINGH-SINGH'S GAUDY BAND OF GUN-RUNNERS RETIRES TO THE HILLS OUTSIDE BLAZE'S STRONGHOLD...
1-27
ORDERS, MASTER?
NO ORDERS! SINK-SINK CAN'T T'INK OF ANYT'INK HURRIBLE ENOFF!
Reg. U. S. Pat. Off.; Copyright, 1940, by News Syndicate Co., Inc.
AFTER DARK, A FIGURE GLIDES THROUGH THE SHADOWS TOWARD THE CAMP FIRES....
WHO YOU?
TELL THE GREAT SINGH-SINGH IT IS A MESSENGER ...WITH INTERESTING NEWS!
MILTON CANIFF

TERRY AND THE PIRATES by MILTON CANIFF
I'LL NEVER FORGET OLD SINGH-SINGH'S FACE WHEN HE SAW THE "BEAUTIFUL AMERICAN GIRL" IN THAT OUTFIT!
DID I DO ALL RIGHT?
YOU WERE TERRIFIC, APRIL! SINGH-SINGH RAN OUT OF HERE AS IF HE HAD INTERCEPTED A PASS! BUT I'M AFRAID OUR TROUBLES ARE JUST BEGINNING!
BLIGH'ME, PATRICK, THEM'S TRUE WORDS! ME DARLIN' DAUGHTER SPILLED IT T' OL' SINGH-SINGH THAT HI AIN'T GOT TH' MONEY T' PAY FER 'IS LOAD O' GUNS!
'E'S BLISTERIN' MAD AT YE FER PULLIN' 'IS LEG — AN' WOT 'E MAY DREAM UP FER REVENGE IS ANY BLOKE'S GUESS!
WELL, BLAZE, YOU RASCAL, GIVING APRIL TO SINGH-SINGH AS A LAST RESORT WAS YOUR ACE IN THE HOLE!... SINCE HE'S PEEVED AT ALL OF US, WE MAY AS WELL STICK TOGETHER!
DON'T BE 'ARD ON ME, PATRICK! ME ONLY DAUGHTER'S UPSTAIRS PLOTTIN' AGAINST US... SINGH-SINGH'S OUT IN THE 'ILLS READY T' STRIKE... HI AIN'T 'APPY — HIF THAT'S ANY SATISFACTION!
NOT MUCH! IF THAT CURIOUS COSSACK GETS NASTY, WE'LL HAVE TO OUTSMART HIM... I'VE GOT A WILD HUNCH THAT MAY DO IT... LISTEN...
MEANWHILE, AT SINGH-SINGH'S CAMP ON THE HILLS NEAR BY....
SINK-SINK IS INSULT! KEPTIN BLAZER DUN'T PAY FOR GONS.... TRY TO GIVE SINK-SINK SCARECROW FOR VIFE! BAH!!
MASTER, COMES MESSENGER!

WHO DIS?
I AM BUT AN HUMBLE WORM, COME WITH INTERESTING NEWS FOR THE MIGHTY SINGH-SINGH!
VELL — SPILL!
THIS UNWORTHY ONE HAS OBSERVED THAT PLANS WERE BEING MADE TO DUPE THE GREAT SINGH-SINGH... BEING AN ADMIRER OF YOUR MAJESTIC SELF, THIS WRETCH HAS TAKEN STEPS TO FOIL THE PLOT...
VOT'S ALL DIS GASSINK? GET TO D' POINT!
CAP'N BLAZE THINKS THAT THE GOLD TO PAY YOU FOR THE SHIPMENT OF GUNS WAS LOST ON THE FLOODED RIVER... IN REALITY I HAVE IT... AND AM READY TO HAND IT OVER TO YOU...
HAW! DOOBLE-CROSS, HUH? SINK-SINK NO CARE WHO GET GONS — SO LONG AS KESH ON LINE! YOU MAD AT BLAZER, NO?
I HATE HIM WITH MAGNIFICENCE! BUT THERE IS MORE... TO FURTHER DISPLACE HIM AS THE AGENT FOR HANDLING YOUR WARES — I CAN COMPLETE THE BARGAIN!!...
YOU MEAN A VIFE FOR SINK-SINK'S HAREM?
YEA! AND ONE WHO SPEAKS ENGLISH! THE GIRL WHO APPEARED BEFORE YOU DRESSED AS A FRIGHTFUL CREATURE IS, IN REALITY, A MOST HANDSOME SPECIMEN! THE DISGUISE WAS TO DISCOURAGE YOUR ATTENTIONS!
1-28
ALL THE GREAT SINGH-SINGH NEED DO IS ATTACK THE WEAK GARRISON — TAKE THE WOMAN-CHILD, AND RETURN TO THE HILLS! IS THIS NOT SO?
IS SO!

SO! YOU DOUBLE-CROSS KEPTIN BLAZER?
HE HAS TREATED THIS PERSON AS A DOG FOR THE LAST TIME! HE THINKS THE GOLD TO PAY FOR YOUR GUNS WAS LOST IN THE RIVER — BUT I HAVE IT! IT IS I WHO WILL DO BUSINESS WITH THE GREAT SINGH-SINGH!...
1-29
...YOU SEE, I EVEN COMPLETE THE BARGAIN... AS I RELATED, THE AMERICAN GIRL WHO APPEARED SO UGLY IS, IN REALITY, QUITE BEAUTIFUL! SHE MAY BE CAPTURED BY A SIMPLE ATTACK ON THE SMALL GARRISON!
AH, IS FACT!
THE REGULAR GATES ARE EASILY DEFENDED — BUT WHEN THE ATTACK IS READY, I WILL OPEN THE SECRET TUNNEL UNDER THE HOUSE — BY THE CREEK! I WILL SIGNAL WITH A LANTERN! I GO NOW, BEFORE I AM MISSED!
BACK IN CAP'N BLAZE'S HOUSE...
SNAP OUT OF IT, BLAZE! IF SINGH-SINGH ATTACKS, WE CAN'T HOLD OUT VERY LONG! WE'LL HAVE TO TRICK HIM! CAN YOU HOOK UP A PUBLIC ADDRESS SYSTEM ON THAT WIRELESS SET OF YOURS?
YEA, THAT HI CAN!... BUT HI DON'T GIT YER IDEA, LAD!
MILTON CANIFF

HERE'S MY HUNCH, BLAZE.... SINGH-SINGH IS GOING TO BE PLENTY BURNED UP AT BOTH OF US...
RIGHT'O, LAD, HI'LL WAGER 'IS MUSTACHE IS CURLIN' FROM TH' 'EAT THIS VERY MINUTE!
1-30
Copyright, 1940, by News Syndicate Co., Inc.
HIS MOB IS CAMPED ON THOSE HILLS... IF WE CAN PLANT LOUD-SPEAKERS NEAR THEIR TENTS, WE MAY BE ABLE TO FRIGHTEN THEM AWAY BY NOISES WE BROADCAST THROUGH YOUR MICROPHONE!
LIKE THE SOUND EFFECTS ON TH' RADIO...
THAT'S RIGHT, KITTEN, WE CAN MAKE THEM THINK THEY'RE BEING ATTACKED BY A TREMENDOUS FORCE... WITH BOMBING PLANES, MACHINE GUNS, AND SO ON...
OH, I READ IN A HONGKONG PAPER 'BOUT A MAN WHO DID THAT ON A PROGRAM BACK HOME... BUT WHAT IF IT FAILS?
...THEN I GUESS WE'LL HAVE TO GO BACK TO MARS!
?
MILTON CANIFF

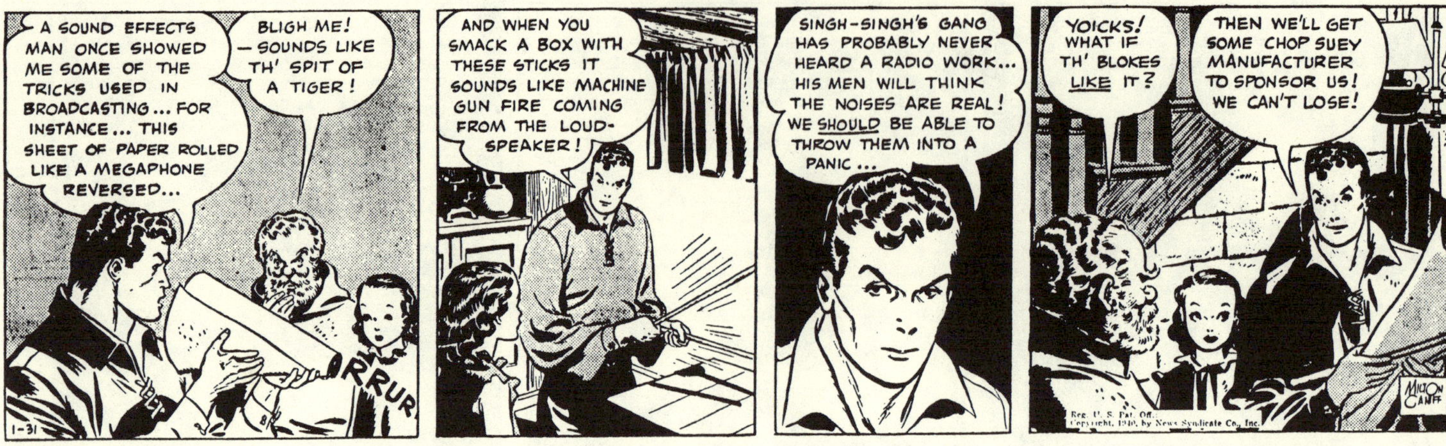
A SOUND EFFECTS MAN ONCE SHOWED ME SOME OF THE TRICKS USED IN BROADCASTING... FOR INSTANCE... THIS SHEET OF PAPER ROLLED LIKE A MEGAPHONE REVERSED...
BLIGH ME! — SOUNDS LIKE TH' SPIT OF A TIGER!
RRUR
1-31
AND WHEN YOU SMACK A BOX WITH THESE STICKS IT SOUNDS LIKE MACHINE GUN FIRE COMING FROM THE LOUD-SPEAKER!
SINGH-SINGH'S GANG HAS PROBABLY NEVER HEARD A RADIO WORK... HIS MEN WILL THINK THE NOISES ARE REAL! WE SHOULD BE ABLE TO THROW THEM INTO A PANIC...
YOICKS! WHAT IF TH' BLOKES LIKE IT?
THEN WE'LL GET SOME CHOP SUEY MANUFACTURER TO SPONSOR US! WE CAN'T LOSE!
MILTON CANIFF

WHAT A FOOL I WAS TO SHOW THAT MAN RYAN I HAVE A WEAKNESS FOR THEATRICALS! HE NEARLY ACCOMPLISHED HIS PURPOSE!
2-1
HE HAD ME RECITE SHAKESPEARE — HOPING SINGH-SINGH WOULD WANT ME FOR HIS ENGLISH-SPEAKING WIFE... BUT EVEN WHEN THAT FAILED, HE HELD A SURPRISE IN RESERVE...
...WHEN I TOLD THAT MONGOLIAN BEAST THERE WAS A BEAUTIFUL AMERICAN GIRL UPSTAIRS, SHE APPEARED IN AN ABSURD MAKEUP! I HAVE BEEN INSULTED AND HUMILIATED... BUT I SHALL ENJOY THE FINAL TRIUMPH...
...REVENGE UPON MY FATHER FOR MY VERY EXISTENCE... UPON RYAN FOR MAKING A FOOL OF ME... AND UPON THE GIRL — BECAUSE SHE IS EVERYTHING I AM NOT! WHAT RELISH THERE IS IN THE CONTEMPLATION OF EVIL! I MUST HURRY!
MILTON CANIFF

2-2
LEFTOVERS FROM LAST YEAR'S OPIUM CROP... NICELY DRIED! THIS IS SO EASY!
SINGH-SINGH, ANGRY AND WAITING OUT IN THE HILLS... ME, ANGRY, BUT NOT WAITING! AN IDEAL COMBINATION FOR DISTRESSING MY FATHER, RYAN, AND THE GIRL!
THE INGREDIENTS ARE AT HAND! ALL I NEED DO IS ADMINISTER MY DEVIL'S BROTH — AND WATCH IT'S EFFECT! I SHOULD NEVER PLAY PORTIA ... LADY MACBETH IS MY TYPE!
MILTON CANIFF

YOU GO TO FRONT GATE — SAY SINK-SINK GIVE KEPTIN BLAZER ONCE MORE CHANCE TO PAY OP!
AYE, SIRE!
2-3
VE GO VAIT FOR SIGNAL FROM ROUND-HEAD!... DEN BUST IN BACK DOOR!
THE BEARDED DOG IS BUSY WITH THE AMERICANS ... SINGH-SINGH WAITS ON THE HILLS! MY MOMENT OF POWER IS AT HAND!
I HAVE THE GOLD TO BUY SINGH-SINGH'S GUNS... AT MY SIGNAL HIS MEN WILL ENTER AND TAKE THE GIRL... AND THE RED DEVIL WILL NO LONGER BE MY MASTER!
MILTON CANIFF

TERRY AND THE PIRATES
by MILTON CANIFF
YOU GET THE IDEA? WE CAN HOLD OLD SINGH-SINGH OFF ONLY SO LONG — BUT BY RIGGING UP THIS PUBLIC ADDRESS SYSTEM WE MAY BE ABLE TO FRIGHTEN HIS CROWD AWAY!
Reg. U. S. Pat. Off.
Copyright, 1940, by News Syndicate Co., Inc.
WE SET UP LOUD SPEAKERS OUT NEAR HIS ARMY — THEN MAKE SOUND EFFECTS NEAR THE MICROPHONE TO SEEM LIKE THEY ARE BEIN' ATTACKED?
THAT'S IT, KITTEN!
MASTER, COME MEN FLOM SINGH-SINGH!... MAKE TALK!
WOT'S THIS 'ERE? MEBBE THE OLD OX WANTS T' CALL A TRUCE! HI'LL GO SEE! LOOK SHARP, PATRICK!
I DON'T LIKE THIS, APRIL! SOUNDS LIKE A TRICK! LOCK YOURSELF IN THIS RADIO ROOM!.... I'M GOING OUTSIDE!
HURRY BACK! I'M SKITTERY!
GUDE! IS LIKE SINGH-SINGH PLAN! IF KEPTIN BLAZER GO TO FRONT GATE... ROUND-HEAD LET US IN SECRET DOOR IN WALL!
BEHOLD! IS SIGNAL LIGHT!
ALL GOES WELL! THE PARLEY AT THE MAIN GATE DIVERTS ATTENTION! ENTER!
WAIT! SOMEONE COMES!
IS IRISHER! SINK-SINK BUST HIS HEAD!
NO, MASTER! AN ALARM WOULD FOR OUR PLAN OF SURPRISE!
IF SINGH-SINGH IS TRYING A TRICK BY DIVERTING BLAZE'S ATTENTION TO THE MAIN GATE, THE ATTACK SHOULD COME FROM BACK HERE!.... HMMM! THOUGHT I HEARD WHISPERS...
MIGHT HAVE BEEN THIS STRONG WIND.... HEY, WHAT'S THAT ODOR? I'VE GOT IT!
PEPPERMINT!!
2-4

GIVE EAR!
NOISE FROM REAR! WE ATTACK!
'EY, YOU BLAWSTED, BLINKIN' BLIGHTERS! HI THOUGHT THIS 'ERE WUZ A PARLEY FER PEACE! IF YE WANTS WAR, YE'LL GIT PLENTY O' SAME! REPEL BOARDERS!
2-5
Reg. U. S. Pat. Off. Copyright, 1940, by News Syndicate Co., Inc.
GIT!
HI 'EAR PATRICK RYAN GIVIN' TONGUE LIKE A PACK O' FOX 'OUNDS! BRING A GANG AN' WE'LL 'OP TO 'IS AID! YAHOO! IF THERE'S ANYTHING HI LIKES BETTER THAN CHECKERS, HIT'S A GOOD BRAWL!
MILTON CANIFF
'OLD FAST, PATRICK! WE'RE COMIN' ALONGSIDE!
SINGH-SINGH'S MOB... SNEAKED IN SOME WAY... I STUMBLED ON THEM...
2-6
NICE STUMBLIN', ME BUCKO! OVERBOARD WITH TH' SCUM!
QUICKLY! OUT THIS WAY! THERE HAS BEEN A MISTAKE!
Reg. U. S. Pat. Off.; Copyright, 1940, by News Syndicate Co., Inc.
SO! AND YOU IS IT!
MILTON CANIFF
OH, GREAT ONE, DO NOT ABANDON ME! THE RED DEVIL WILL KILL ME! REMEMBER, I HAVE THE GOLD!
IS FACT! COME ON, DUMB-HEAD!
2-7
SINK-SINK IS MAD!!
AND I CANNOT BLAME YOU, GREAT ONE! THERE WILL BE NO SATISFACTION UNTIL THE RED DOG IS CRUSHED!
OUR MISADVENTURE WAS SIMPLY ILL LUCK! THE GARRISON IS NOT HEAVILY ARMED! ATTACK IN FORCE AND YOU WILL WIN EASILY!
Reg. U. S. Pat. Off.; Copyright, 1940, by News Syndicate Co., Inc.
DIS TIME SINK-SINK CATCH KEPTIN BLAZER AN' DAT IRISHER—VE HANG 'EM BY FEET AN' SWING 'EM INTO EACH OTHER TILL HEADS IS BUST!
DELIGHTFUL! AND THIS TIME I WILL GO PERSONALLY AND CAPTURE THE PRETTY AMERICAN GIRL! I WILL ONLY HURT HER A LITTLE TINY BIT!
MILTON CANIFF
THAT CLEANS 'EM OUT, BLAZE, BUT THIS ISN'T THE END!... CUE-BALL AND SINGH-SINGH, HIMSELF, WERE IN THAT MOB! THE OLD BOY WILL BE HOPPIN' MAD!
YE SPEAK TRUE, LAD!—SO CUE-BALL TURNED TRAITOR... THAT'S 'OW THEY GOT IN ME SECRET TUNNEL UNDER THE WALL! THAT BALD-'EADED BILGE RAT!
2-8
Reg. U. S. Pat. Off. Copyright, 1940, by News Syndicate Co., Inc.
WE CAN EXPECT A MASS ATTACK NOW! WE'LL SEE WHETHER THE LOUD-SPEAKER STUNT WILL WORK! LET'S GET IT SET UP!
BLIGH'ME, IF THAT FAILS, WE'LL 'AVE T' SCATTER PAMPHLETS!
MEANWHILE: IN CHEERY'S ROOM....
SO! MY HONORABLE PARENT AND THAT MAN RYAN SEEM TO HAVE HALTED SINGH-SINGH FOR THE MOMENT...
BUT SINGH-SINGH DID NOT HAVE MY HELP.... HE WILL RETURN— AND BY THEN MY BREW WILL BE COOKED!
..."DOUBLE, DOUBLE TOIL AND TROUBLE; FIRE BURN AND CAULDRON BUBBLE..." HA! WHAT SPORT!!
MILTON CANIFF

I WAS FRANTIC WHEN I HEARD TH' SHOUTIN' AN' SHOOTIN' DURIN' TH' NIGHT! WHAT HAPPENS NOW, MISTER RYAN?

SINGH-SINGH WILL HARDLY ATTACK IN DAYLIGHT...

SOON AS IT'S DUSK, I'LL GO OUT AND SET UP THE LOUD-SPEAKERS... THEN WE'LL KEEP A DOGWATCH IN SHIFTS TO AVOID SURPRISE!

THIS SUSPENSE WILL HAVE ME FIT T'SWOON! WHAT DO I DO?

WHEN YOU'RE NOT WITH ME, STAY LOCKED IN THIS ROOM! WE DON'T KNOW WHO BESIDES CUE-BALL MAY BE A TRAITOR!

BY THE WAY... WHERE'S THAT SCREWY SERVANT NAMED TWIDDLE-WIT?

OH, I RECKON HE'S PUTTERIN' ABOUT SOMEWHERE! MY CHIEF THOUGHT JUS' NOW IS HOW I CAN COAX THOSE BUTTERFLIES T'STOP FLITTIN' 'ROUND IN MY TUMMY!

GETTING DARK! I'M OFF TO SET UP THE LOUD-SPEAKERS! IF I HAVE TROUBLE, I'LL RUN FOR IT! HAVE THE SENTRIES COVER ME WITH MACHINE GUNS!

TH' WHOLE BLINKIN' CREW IS SO JITTERY THEY'LL LIKELY POT YE, PATRICK! GOOD SAILIN', ME BUCKO!

MEANWHILE: IN THE KITCHEN OF CAP'N BLAZE'S ESTABLISHMENT....

PERFECT! THE COOKS STAND ABOUT IN EXCITED GROUPS! THIS WILL BE SIMPLE!

TINCTURE OF OPIUM ADDED TO THE EVENING CURRY.... THE COLOR BLENDS.... AND THERE IS NO TASTE... BUT THE EFFECT WILL BE FASCINATING TO SEE!

HA! IT IS DONE – AND I WAS NOT DISCOVERED! NOW SINGH-SINGH MAY WALK IN AND VENT HIS WRATH ON MY FATHER, RYAN AND THE GIRL! THERE IS ONLY ONE THING.... WHEN THIS PLACE FALLS – WHAT HAPPENS TO ME?

TERRY
AND THE PIRATES
by MILTON CANIFF

LUCK SO FAR... IF I CAN GET THESE LOUD SPEAKERS UP BEFORE SINGH-SINGH TRIES A SECOND ATTACK WE MAY BE ABLE TO SCARE HIM OFF!

WITH CUE-BALL TURNED TRAITOR WE CAN'T TRUST ANYONE! BLAZE, APRIL AND I WILL HAVE TO PUT ON OUR SOUND EFFECTS STUNT ALONE!

YE MADE HIT, LAD! WE 'AD YE COVERED, BUT HI SHOOK IN ME BOOTS!

PLENTY TO SHAKE ABOUT! SINGH-SINGH'S MOB IS FORMING FOR A MASS ATTACK... THAT'S WHY THEY DIDN'T NOTICE ME! THE OLD BOY WILL BE BOUNCIN' MAD AFTER HIS LAST FAILURE!

I TOLD APRIL TO STAY LOCKED IN HER ROOM EXCEPT WHEN SHE'S NEAR ME! BETTER FEED THE GARRISON WELL BEFORE THINGS START TO POP!

RIGHT'O! WHERE'S THAT TWIDDLE-WIT SERVANT? 'E MUST BE 'IDIN' SOMEWHERE, QUAKIN' SCARED... HI'LL ORDER MESS MESELF!

THEY'RE CARRYING FOOD TO THE SENTRIES ON THE WALL... AND THE OTHERS MUST BE EATING IN THE BARRACKS! THEY DO NOT KNOW THERE IS AN EXTRA INGREDIENT IN THAT CURRIED RICE!...

...FOR I AM HAVING MY REVENGE ON MY FATHER, RYAN AND THE GIRL! I MADE A TINCTURE OF DRIED OPIUM AND POURED IT INTO THE STEAMING KETTLES! IN A SHORT TIME THE GARRISON WILL BE FOGGED WITH DREAMS....
...THEN SINGH-SINGH AND HIS MEN MAY WALK IN AND DO AS THEY LIKE! THEY WILL TORTURE ALL BUT THE GIRL... SHE MAY LOOK FORWARD TO A LIFETIME IN SINGH-SINGH'S HAREM....
...ONLY ONE POSSIBILITY I FAILED TO CONSIDER IN MY PLAN!... WHAT HAPPENS TO ME WHEN SINGH-SINGH TAKES OVER?
AS THE GREAT ONE KNOWS, THERE IS A LIGHT BARBED WIRE FENCE ON THE APPROACHABLE SIDE OF THE ENCLOSURE.... THEN THE WALL! ARE THE SCALING LADDERS READY?
SHOO! DIS TIME NO SECRET DOORS! VE BUST 'EM ON NOSE!
KEPTIN BLAZER EXPECT ATTACK AT DAWN – VE GO AT MIDNIGHTS! VE SMACK HIM- AN' IRISHER TO PIECES!
SPLENDID! AND I WILL SEE THAT THE PRETTY AMERICAN GIRL IS RETURNED TO YOU! THEY WILL PLACE HER IN HER ROOM, THINKING IT IS THE SAFEST HAVEN DURING A BATTLE!
2-11
I AM QUITE FILLED! OUR MASTER FEEDS US WELL ON THE EVE OF BATTLE!
AYE! BUT WITH THE SENSE OF WELL-BEING COMES A GREAT DROWSINESS!
THE MEN ON THE WALLS 'AVE BEEN SERVED AT THEIR POSTS... AN' THE RESERVES ARE EATIN' IN TH' BARRACKS! WE'D BETTER STOKE UP TOO, PATRICK!
RIGHT! IT'LL BE A LONG NIGHT!
2-12
SAY, HE SET APRIL'S PLACE! I THINK SHE'D BETTER STAY IN HER ROOM!
HI'LL 'AVE TWIDDLE-WIT TAKE 'ERS UP TO 'ER! TWIDDLE-WIT!
Reg. U. S. Pat. Off.: Copyright, 1940, by News Syndicate Co., Inc.
WHERE IS THAT NO-GOOD? ...BLAWSTED 'EATHENS AIN'T EVER ABOUT WHEN THEY'RE NEEDED!
DON'T BOTHER! I'LL TAKE HER FOOD UPSTAIRS! SHE'S NERVOUS ...I'LL TRY TO CALM HER DOWN A BIT!
OH, MISTER RYAN, IT WAS MIGHTY THOUGHTFUL OF YOU T' CARRY MY DINNER HERE, BUT I SWEAR I CAN'T EAT A SPECK!
OH, SURE YOU CAN, KITTEN! CAN'T FIGHT ON AN EMPTY STOMACH! PITCH IN!
MILTON CANIFF
HERE I SIT GABBIN' AN' EATIN' – WHILE YOUR FOOD'S GETTIN' COLD DOWNSTAIRS! YOU RUN NOW! I'LL BE ALL RIGHT!
PLENTY MORE IN THE KITCHEN! LOCK YOURSELF IN WHEN I LEAVE, SUGAH!
2-13
...BUILDING'S QUIET AS A TOMB! WOULDN'T THINK WE'RE EXPECTING AN ATTACK TONIGHT!
SAY, BLAZE--- HMMM... THE OLD BOY'S ASLEEP! JUST AS WELL... HE'LL NEED THE REST! I WON'T ROUSE HIM!
Reg. U. S. Pat. Off.: Copyright, 1940, by News Syndicate Co., Inc.
THIS CURRY IS COLD... BETTER CALL THE BOY AND GET A HOT DISH! I'LL NEED THE ENERGY!...
MILTON CANIFF

OTHER CANIFF BOOKS FROM NBM

TERRY & THE PIRATES "COLLECTORS' EDITION"
12 288-320 page, hardbound, gold stamped books reprint the complete *TERRY*. Every daily and Sunday strip, many never before reprinted, is shown in full size. Write for more information.

MILTON CANIFF - REMBRANDT OF THE COMIC STRIP
The original version of this book appeared in 1946 as Caniff was finishing his work on *TERRY*. Comic historian Rick Marschall has updated this 1980 edition. There are many rare and beautiful illustrations and blowups of Caniff art. Paperback - $6.95.

MISSING ANY VOLUMES?
TERRY & THE PIRATES paperback reprinting chronologically from the beginning. Issued quarterly. Each 64 pp., 8 1/2x11, color cover.
Vol. 1 Welcome to China (1934) $5.95
Vol. 2 Marooned with Burma (1935) $5.95
Vol. 3 Dragon Lady's Revenge (1936) $5.95
Vol. 4 Getting Snared (1936-1937) $5.95
Vol. 5 Shanghaied (1937) $5.95
Vol. 6 The Warlord Klang (1937-1938) $6.95
Vol. 7 The Hunter (1938) $6.95
Vol. 8 The Baron (1938-1939) $6.95
Vol. 9 Feminine Venom (1939) $6.95
Vol. 10 Network of Intrigue (1939-1940) $6.95

NOW AVAILABLE: SUBSCRIPTIONS!
You can subscribe to 4 starting with any volume: $25 (free P&H).

ALSO: HANDSOME SLIPCASED SETS
4 Volumes in each for a total of 256 pages of intense reading slipcased in beautiful leatherette, gold stamped.
Vols. 1-4: $27.50
Vols. 5-8: $29.50
slipcase alone: $7.50

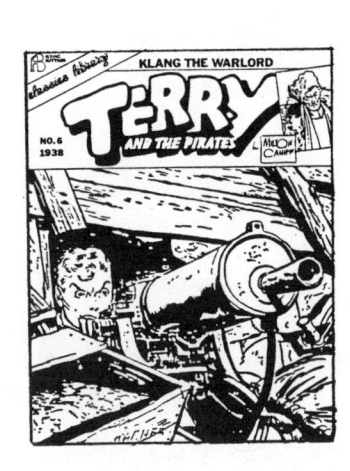

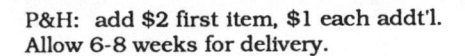

P&H: add $2 first item, $1 each addt'l.
Allow 6-8 weeks for delivery.

NBM
35-53 70th St.
Jackson Heights, NY 11372

Flying Buttress Classics Library
announces:

the complete

WASH TUBBS & CAPTAIN EASY

by **ROY CRANE**

1924 – 1943

The *Flying Buttress Classics Library*, announces a new reprint: Roy Crane's classic *WASH TUBBS* (1924-1943). Wash Tubbs was Crane's first strip, and already with it he set the pace for future adventure strips to match, including Terry & The Pirates. Wash Tubbs exemplifies two-fisted adventure spiced with a good sense of humor. Wash and his pals, Gozzy Gallup and **Captain Easy**, battle arch villians Bull Dawson and Shanghai Slug in exotic locales on land and sea around the world.

Each volume of this quarterly **18 volume complete reprint** will contain 192 pages of action. Like our recently completed Terry & The Pirates series, you can count on high quality and regular publishing schedules. Both hardcover and paperback will be available in a large but handy 11 by 8 1/2 format. Each volume will print approximately one year's worth of strips. Sundays are included.

PAPERBACK EDITION:
$16.95 each
(add $2.00 postage & handling)

HARDCOVER EDITION
$32.50 each
(add $2.00 postage & handling)

Vols. 1-5 available

SEVEN CENTURIES AGO GHENGIS KHAN AND HIS HORDE OF SAVAGE MONGOLS OVER-RAN ALL CHINA.

SPECIAL OFFER:
Order your subscription to any 4 hardcover volumes and pay only $80!
Also available: you can subscribe to the paperback edition for $50 for any four. (no p + h for subs)

NBM
35-53 70th St.
Jackson Heights, NY 11372